FROEBE[L]
BY KATE DO[UGLAS]
AND NORA ARC[HIBALD]

Available online at HTTP:
www.gutenberg.org/files/31097-h/31097-h.htm The republic of childhood

Douglas-Wiggin, K. and Archibald Smith, N. (1895) (1895)
Vol 1 Froebels Gifts, Reviveside Press, Cambridge.

Reviveside press, H.O. Houghton Massachusett, USA Houghton and Company

PREFACE

The three little volumes on that Republic of Childhood, the kindergarten, of which this handbook, dealing with the gifts, forms the initial number, might well be called Chips from a Kindergarten Workshop. They are the outcome of talks and conferences on Froebel's educational principles with successive groups of earnest young women here, there, and everywhere, for fifteen years, and represent as much practical work at the bench as a carpenter could show in a similar length of time. They are the result of mutual give and take, of question and answer, of effort and experience, of the friction of minds against one another, of ideas struck out in the heat of argument, and of varied experience with many hundred little children of all nationalities and conditions. They are not theories, written in the seclusion of the study; and if perchance they have the defects, so should they have the virtues, [Pg vi]too, of work corrected and revised at every step by the "child in the midst." If it is objected that many things in them have been heard before, we can but say with Montaigne: "Truth and reason are common to every one, and are no more his who spake them first than his who spake them after."

The various talks have been cut down here, enlarged there, condensed in one place, amplified in another, from year to year, as knowledge and experience have grown; many of the ideas which they advocated in the beginning have been eliminated, as being completely reversed by the passage of time, and much new matter has been added as the kindergarten principle has developed. They are as much a growth as a coral reef, though the authors have little hope that they will be as enduring.

The kindergarten of 1895 is not the kindergarten of 1880, for the science of education has made great strides in these past fifteen years. Many things which were held to be vital principles when we began our talks with kindergarten students, we now find were but lifeless methods after all. It is not that time has reversed the fundamental principles on which the kindergarten [Pg vii]rests,—these are as true as truth and as changeless; but the interpretation of them has greatly changed and broadened with the passage of years, and many of the instrumentalities of education which Froebel devised are destined to further transformation in the future. For this reason, the last book on the kindergarten is sometimes the best book, since it naturally embodies the latest thought and discovery on the subject.

These talks on the kindergarten have purposely been divested of a certain amount of technicality and detail, in the hope that they will thus reach not only kindergarten students, but the many mothers and teachers who really long to know what Froebel's system of education is and what it aims to do. They will never of themselves make a kindergartner, and are not intended to do so; but they certainly should shed some light on Froebel's theories, and establish a basis on which they can be worked out in the home and in the school.

We shall attempt no defense of the kindergarten here. It has passed the experimental stage; it is no longer on trial for its life; and no longer humbly begging, hat in hand, for a place to lay its head. As an educational idea, it is a recognized [Pg viii]part of the great system of child-training; and to say, in this year of our Lord, one thousand eight hundred and ninety-five, that one does not believe in the kindergarten is as if one said, I do not believe in electricity, or, I never saw much force in the law of gravitation.

True, Froebel's ideas are often misinterpreted and misapplied; often espoused by ignorant and sentimental persons; often degraded in their practical application; true, the ideal kindergarten and the ideal kindergartner are seldom seen—(though they are worth traveling a thousand miles *to* see)—all this is true, and no one knows it better than we; but that a divine idea is wrongly used does not invalidate its divinity.

That kindergarten principles are gaining ground everywhere; that every year more free and private kindergartens are established, more training schools opened, more students applying for instruction, more books written on the subject, more educational periodicals seeking for kindergarten articles, more cities adding it to their school systems, more normal schools giving courses in kindergarten training, more mothers and teachers seeking for light on Froebel's principles,—all these are matters of statistics which any one may [Pg ix]verify by consulting the Reports of the Commissioner of Education and the various educational magazines.

Our modest volumes, of which the second will deal with the occupations, the third with the educational theories of Froebel, do not claim to be deeply philosophic, nor even to be exhaustive. They are, in a sense, what is called a "popular" treatise on a scientific subject; and though some scientists decry such treatises, yet there are many persons to whom a simple message carries more conviction than a purely philosophic one.

It is hoped that the psychologic principles on which the talks rest are at least measurably correct, though when doctors disagree on vital points, how shall the layman know the extent of his own ignorance?

The authors have always been of a humble and docile spirit, and in the earlier years of their work with children, looking upon all treatises on education as inspired, tried faithfully to make the child's mind work according to the laws therein laid down. But sometimes the child's mind obstinately declined to follow the prescribed route; it refused to begin at the proper beginning of a subject and go on logically to the end, as the books decreed, but flew into the middle of it, and darted both ways, like a weaver's shuttle. If, then, any one of the theories we enunciate does not coincide with your particular educational creed, we can only say that ours, we fear, has sometimes been a "rule of thumb" psychology, and that in our experience it has occasionally been necessary to turn a psychologic law the other end foremost before it could be made to fit the child.

We have endeavored not to be dogmatic in any of these talks, for we do not claim to have seen and counted all the facets of the crystal of truth. We humbly acknowledge that we have often been wrong in the past, and no reason has latterly been given us to believe ourselves infallible; but these disputed points in the kindergarten are, after all, of no more vital importance than the old theologic controversy as to how many angels can stand on the point of a needle. If the occupations are found to be based on incorrect psychologic principles, do not use them; if a similar objection is made to the gifts, substitute others. These are all accessories,—they are of no more importance than the leaves to the tree; if time and stress of weather strip them off, the life current is still there, and new ones will grow in their places.

Kate Douglas Wiggin.
Nora Archibald Smith.

August, 1895.

FROEBEL'S GIFTS
THOUGHTS ON THE GIFTS OF FROEBEL

"A correct comprehension of external, material things is a preliminary to a just comprehension of intellectual relations."

Friedrich Froebel.

"The A, B, C of things must precede the A, B, C of words, and give to the words (abstractions) their true foundations. It is because these foundations fail so often in the present time that there are so few men who think independently and express skillfully their inborn divine ideas."

Friedrich Froebel.

"Perception is the beginning and the preliminary condition for thinking. One's own perceptions awaken one's own conceptions, and these awaken one's own thinking in later stages of development. Let us have no precocity, but natural, that is consecutive, development."

Friedrich Froebel.

"Every child brings with him into the world the natural disposition to see correctly what is before him, or, in other words, the truth. If things are shown to him in their connection, his soul perceives them thus as a conception. But if, as often happens, things are brought before his mind singly, or piecemeal, and in fragments, then the natural disposition to see correctly is perverted to the opposite, and the healthy mind is perplexed."

Friedrich Froebel.

"The linking together which is everywhere seen, and which holds the Universe in its wholeness and unity, the eye receives, and thereby receives the representation, but without understanding it except as an impression and an image. But these first impressions are the root-fibres for the understanding that is developed later."

Friedrich Froebel.

"The correct perception is a preparation for correct knowing and thinking."

Friedrich Froebel.

"No new subject of instruction should come to the scholar, of which he does not at least conjecture that it is grounded in the former subject, and how it is so grounded as its application shows, and concerning which he does not, however dimly, feel it to be a need of the human spirit."

Friedrich Froebel.

"The sequences which the child builds, as well as the sequence of the kindergarten gifts, point on the one hand to physical evolution, wherein each form 'remembers the next inferior and predicts the next higher,' and on the other to the process of historic development, which magnifies the present by linking with it the past and the future."

Susan E. Blow.

"Let us educate the senses, train the faculty of speech, the art of receiving, storing, and expressing impressions, which is the natural gift of infants, and we shall not need books to fill up the emptiness of our teaching until the child is at least seven years old."

E. Seguin.

"As soon as we, young or old, have taken to the habit of asking the book for what it is in our power to learn from personal observation, we dismiss our organs of perception and comprehension from their righteous charge, and cover the emptiness of our own minds with the patchwork of others."

E. SEGUIN.

"Natural geometry (taking the word in its limited sense of study of form in space) is the object of a desire which generally precedes the artificial curiosity for the meaning of letters."

E. SEGUIN.

"Without an accurate acquaintance with the visible and tangible properties of things, our conceptions must be erroneous, our inferences fallacious, and our operations unsuccessful."

HERBERT SPENCER.

"The truths of number, of form, of relationship in position, were all originally drawn from [Pg 4]objects; and to present these truths to the child in the concrete is to let him learn them as the race learned them."

HERBERT SPENCER.

"If we consider it, we shall find that exhaustive observation is an element of all great success."

HERBERT SPENCER.

"Learn to comprehend each thing in its entire history. This is the maxim of science guided by the reason."

WM. T. HARRIS.

"Geometrical facts and conceptions are easier to a child than those of arithmetic."

THOMAS HILL.

"Instruction must begin with actual inspection, not with verbal descriptions of things. From such inspection it is that certain knowledge comes. What is actually seen remains faster in the memory than description or enumeration a hundred times as often repeated."

COMENIUS.

"Observation is the absolute basis of all knowledge. The first object, then, in education, must be to lead the child to observe with accuracy; the second, to express with correctness the results of his observation."

PESTALOZZI.

"If in the external universe any one constructive principle can be detected, it is the geometrical."

BULWER-LYTTON.

"The education of the senses neglected, all after-education partakes of a drowsiness, a haziness, [Pg 5]an insufficiency, which it is impossible to cure."

LORD BACON.

"Of this thing be certain: Wouldst thou plant for eternity? Then plant into the deep infinite faculties of man, his fantasy and heart. Wouldst thou plant for year and day? Then plant into his shallow, superficial faculties, his self-love, and arithmetical understanding, what will grow there."

THOS. CARLYLE.

THE BALL

[Pg 6]

FROEBEL'S FIRST GIFT

"I wish to find the right forms for awakening the higher senses of the child: what symbol does my ball offer to him? That of unity."

"The ball connects the child with nature as much as the universe connects man with God."

FRIEDRICH FROEBEL.

"Line in nature is not found, Unit and Universe are round."

"Nature centres into balls."

R. W. EMERSON.

"From thy handThe worlds were cast; yet every leaflet claimsFrom that same hand its little shining sphereOf starlit dew."

O. W. HOLMES.

"The Small, a sphere as perfect as the GreatTo the soul's absoluteness."

ROBERT BROWNING.

1. The first gift consists of six soft woolen balls colored in the six standard colors derived from the spectrum, namely, red, orange, yellow, green, blue, and violet.

The balls should be provided with strings for use in the various motions.[1]

2. Froebel chose the ball as the first gift because it is the simplest shape, and the one from which all others may subsequently be derived; [Pg 7]the shape most easily grasped by the hand as well as by the mind. It is an object which attracts by its pleasing color, and one which, viewed from all directions, ever makes the same impression.[2]

3. The most important characteristics of the gift are Unity, Activity, Color.

The various colors serve to distinguish these several playmates of the child by special characteristics, and enable him to make his first clear analyses or abstractions, since the color is the only point wherein the objects differ. This contrast in color results in the abstraction of color from form.

4. Since the ball is the most mobile of inanimate shapes, it may be considered as the "opposite equal" of the living organism. The quickness and ease of its motion as well as its elasticity cause the child to regard it as instinct with life, while its softness renders him able to grasp and handle it readily.

Its material is also of great advantage in that it lessens the possibility of startling noises which would distract the child from the contemplation of its qualities. By its use, he is first led to observation, and then to self-expression. As the [Pg 8]simplest type-form as well as the most universal, it offers a satisfactory basis for the classification of objects in general; while its indefiniteness and adaptability make it a useful medium for the expression of the child's vague ideas. With the ball we give first impressions of *Unity, Form, Color, Material, Mobility, Motion, Direction,* and *Position.* The ball songs and plays are used as the first exercises in language, singing, and rhythm.

5. As the kindergarten gifts are designed to serve as an alphabet of form, by whose use the child may learn to read all material objects, it follows that they must form an organically connected sequence, moving in logical order from an object which contains all qualities, but directly emphasizes none, to objects more specialized in nature, and therefore more definitely suggestive as to use.

"Each successive gift in the series must not only be implicit in, but demanded by, its predecessor;" so Froebel selects the ball, with its simplicity but great adaptability, for the starting-point of his series.

6. Connected contrasts of Motion, Direction, and Position are shown in the first gift. By the use of pigments, the so-called secondary colors, purple, orange, and green, may be produced from the opposite hues, red and blue, red and yellow, and blue and yellow.

[Pg 9]"The mind is aroused to attention and led to comparison by contrasts; on the groundwork of comparison, it is enabled to do the work of classification, of clear abstraction, of the formation of definite ideas by the connection of these contrasts."[3]

The Ball a Universal Plaything.

"The presentiment of truth always goes before the recognition of it," says Froebel; and it would seem, indeed, as it, in selecting the first gift, he looked far back into the past of humanity, and there sought the thread which from the beginning connects all times and leads to the farthest future.

"The ball is the last plaything of men, as well as the first with children." In Kreutzer's "Symbolik" we read that the educators of the young god Bacchus gave him golden balls to play [Pg 10]with, and also that the youthful princes of Persia played with them, and alone had this privilege.

It is a significant fact that we find balls even among the remains of the Lake Dwellers of Northern Italy and Switzerland, while small, round balls, resembling marbles, have been found in the early Egyptian tombs. The Teutons made ball-plays national, and built houses in which to indulge in these exercises in all sections of Germany, as late as the close of the sixteenth century. The ancient Aztecs used the game of ball as a training in warfare for the young men of the nation; and that it was considered of great importance is evident from the fact that the tribute exacted by a certain Aztec monarch from some of the cities conquered by him consisted of balls, and amounted to sixteen thousand annually.

The ball entered into many of the favorite games alike of the Greeks and the Romans, the former having a special place in their gymnasiums and a special master for it. It may be noted also that nearly all our modern sports are based upon the effort to get possession of a ball.

Froebel's Ideas of First Gift.

Froebel considered the ball as an external counterpart of the child in the first stages of his development, its undivided unity corresponding to his mental condition, and its movableness to his instinctive activity. Through its recognition he is led to separate [Pg 11]himself from the external world, and the external world from himself.[4]

Froebel's intention was that the first gift should be used in the nursery,[5] but as this is for the most part neglected, or imperfectly and unwisely done, we begin the series of kindergarten play-lessons with it, illustrating its qualities and asking questions concerning them, always diversifying the exercises with rhymes, games, and songs. We must remember that to the young child, as to primitive man, the activity of an object is more pleasing than its qualities, and we should therefore devise a series of games with the fascinating plaything which will lead the child to learn these qualities by practical experience.

Manner of Introduction.

Before beginning any exercise we should fully decide in our own minds the main point or points to be brought out,—Color, Form, or Direction, for example; then, and only then, will the child gain a clear, definite impression, [Pg 12]and have a distinct remembrance of what we have been trying to teach. By way of diversion, every song or rhyme in which the ball can play a symbolic part in action, and illustrate the point we wish to make, is of use in the lessons.[6]

With this dainty colored plaything we begin our first bit of education,—not instruction, mere pouring in, but true education, drawing out, developing. The balls should be kept in a pretty basket, as the beautiful should be cultivated in every way in the true kindergarten; and when they are given to the class, it should be with some little song sung by the kindergartner or one of the older children. At the close of the lesson, as the basket is passed, each child may gently drop his ball into it, saying simply, "Thank you for my ball," or naming its color. At other times they may be called by the names of fruits or flowers, the child saying, "I will give you a cherry," or, "I will give you a violet."

Method of Introduction.

The qualities of the ball must of course be brought before the child's observation in some more or less definite order, and it will be profitable to consider the relative claims of Form and Color to the first place.

We might say, correctly, that to illustrate the [Pg 13]ball, we should begin with its essential qualities.[7] The essential quality is Unity. Unity depends on Form, and the ball's form never changes; therefore we might conclude that this should be the first subject under consideration, since we always treat of the universal properties of objects before special ones, proceeding from homogeneous to heterogeneous. This view of the subject is supported by Ratich's important maxim, "First the thing, and then its properties."

Conrad Diehl.

On the other hand, Conrad Diehl says: "Color is the first sensation of which an infant is capable. With the first ray of light that enters the retina of the eye, the presence of color forces itself on the mind.... When light is present, color is present. The first impression which the eye receives of an object is its color; its form is revealed by the action of light upon its surfaces. We recognize at a distance the color of a leaf, an apple, a flower or berry, long before we are able distinctly to make out their forms. In the absence of light, neither the color nor the form of an object can be seen."[8]

Herbert Spencer.

[Pg 14]Spencer says:[9] "The earliest impressions which the mind can assimilate are those given to it by the undecomposable sensations, resistance, light, sound, etc. Manifestly decomposable states of consciousness cannot exist before the states of consciousness out of which they are composed. There can be no idea of form until some familiarity with light in its gradations and qualities, or resistance in its different intensities, has been acquired; for, as has long been known, we recognize visible form by means of varieties of light, and tangible form by means of varieties of resistance. Similarly, no articulate sound is cognizable until the inarticulate sounds which go to make it up have been learned. And thus must it be in every other case."[10]

Froebel.

The balance of authority seems to be, on the whole, upon the side of presenting color first to the young child, as we appeal to the emotions at this age rather than to the intellect; and while the senses revel in color, form follows more the law of use. Let us hear, however, what the "great pioneer of child study" says upon this point. Froebel says, as distinct and different as color and form may be in [Pg 15]themselves, they are to the young child indivisible, as inseparable as body and life. Nay, the idea of color seems to come to the child, as perhaps to mankind in general, through the forms; so, on the other hand, the forms gain prominence and impressiveness by the colors. Hence ideas of colors must at first be coupled with ideas of form, and *vice versa*; color and form are in the beginning an undivided unity.[11]

The color and form of the ball being indissolubly blended in the child's eyes, we can scarcely teach them separately at first. We may, however, consider each by itself, in order to present the subject more clearly.

FORM.

Form.

To teach form in an interesting manner, to make it plain to the child without giving him any terms, but rather coaxing him by ingenuity to formulate his own knowledge, is a difficult thing to do, and should not [Pg 16]be attempted at all with very young children. It seems unnecessary to say that Froebel did not intend the ball should be made a medium of object lessons for babies, although this distorted view of his idea seems to have entered the minds of some critics.

The child, when old enough to enter a kindergarten, will generally know round objects, and be somewhat familiar with the ball already in his home plays. We should let him roll and grasp it in his tiny fingers, till gradually, in comparison with other objects handled in the same way, he notices the absence of corners, edges, or any obstructions which would meet his touch or eye. Then we may ask him if he could make a ball out of a rough block of wood which we show. Some bright little one will guess that a carpenter could do it with his tools. "What would he have to do?" "Plane it off," will perhaps be the answer. "Where and how is he to plane?" may be the next inquiry, and the child often answers, "All the rough parts and the parts that stick out." "Why does he like to play ball?" He does not know exactly. "Would he like to play ball with the scissors?" "Why not?" "Then why does he like to feel the ball in his hand?"

After such preliminary conversations upon the form of the ball, we may lead the children first to note other round things in the room, and then to recall what they have at home of a similar [Pg 17]shape and what they may have seen in the streets. These exercises are always delightful to the little ones, and are invaluable to the kindergartner, as they furnish a thorough test of the child's comprehension of the subject she has been handling.[12] We should notice slight divergences from the spherical form in the objects the children name, and speak of them. They will soon be able to tell in every case where the egg or cobblestone is not "just round."

They will of course mention stove-lids, dinner-plates, etc., as round objects, and the attempt to give a clear and definite understanding of the difference between solids and planes is difficult at first, but they very soon discriminate between rounding objects that possess thickness and those that are flat but have curved edges. A ball of putty or one of dough is a good thing with which to illustrate this difference.

We must remember that any abstract teaching on Form is too difficult at this time, much more [Pg 18]difficult than Color. Let the children, during these first few weeks, draw circles on the blackboard and on paper, and sew, and draw pictures of balls, peaches, or round fruits; they may also make balls of wax, dough, or clay. Rousseau says, "A child may forget what he sees, and sooner still what is said to him, but he never forgets what he has made."

COLOR.

Color.

"The comprehension of the single tone of color gradually leads to the comprehension of the full chord; the recognition of single colors leads to the recognition of shades and their harmonious connections: thus, step by step, the capacity of comprehending nature in its beauty and with its treasures is developed."[13]

Again, suppose the play-lesson for the day to be upon Color. Of course, the subject may be handled in a dozen different ways and serve for a dozen different lessons; a few hints only are here given, as in matters of detail it is better that each teacher should be free and unguided in the use of her own ingenuity.

We may take, perhaps, the red[14] ball, and, holding [Pg 19]it high in the air, ask, "Who has a ball exactly like mine? Look carefully, now, and then show me." A volley of balls, comprising every color in the rainbow, will be shot into the air, and then becomes necessary the task of discrimination. We may find the red ones, and gratify the children by naming those who possess them, as it seems a great honor in their eyes. Now they should be led to find every bit of red in the room,—Andrew's stockings, Mary's ribbon, the tiny pipings on Katie's apron, Jim's necktie, your belt, the flowers on the wall, etc. The scene will become intensely exciting; the bright eyes will begin searching in every corner of the room, and the transport which will greet us when anything far out of sight and of the right color is discovered is truly refreshing.

All the children, as far as possible, should be engaged in this diversion, while the most timid and backward should be kept near and encouraged with word and smile. The name of the color should not be asked for, or given, till it can be matched by all, and found in surrounding objects.

We may ask what flowers they have seen which were like the color they are studying, and show them some of the more familiar kinds; also speak of the action of the sun in making certain fruits red,—the raspberries and strawberries, for instance. Some rosy-faced little urchin in the class may be chosen and asked how he keeps such [Pg 20]red cheeks, and from this the idea of red as the color of warmth and life may be developed. We may proceed with blue and yellow, then with violet, orange, and green, in like manner, constantly diversifying the exercises with plays, songs, and appropriate stories.

Hints on Additional Color Exercises.

The formation of the so-called secondary colors will not be very obvious to the younger children, nor is the fact to be taught scientifically or learned by them; they will, however, be greatly interested in the mixing of paints in small dishes, or the blending of different colored crayons on the blackboard.

Red and *Yellow* into *Orange*.
Yellow and *Blue* into *Green*.
Blue and *Red* into *Purple*.

Pieces of glass are serviceable objects with which to show the same thing, or we can buy the "gelatine films" from any kindergarten supply store. Holding the red and yellow, one on the other, for instance, the piece nearer the eye will, of course, determine the shade; if the red piece be next the eye, the orange color will be deeper than if the yellow were in the same position. None of these experiments, however, will produce pure colors, the green and purple being especially unsatisfactory.

Among the devices with which to teach color may be recommended a color quilt made of various shades and shapes of woolens and silks or [Pg 21]ribbons. This may be used as a sort of chart, to the great delight of the children, and is one of the valuable aids in teaching, because it calls out both individual and general action. We may also make a clothes-line of twine and suspend it from door to door, or between any two suitable points, attaching to it pieces of all colors, and, after a while, of various tints and shades of worsted, letting the children touch the ones designated, or find bits of the same color as their balls.

Cards wound with different tints and shades of the same color are also useful when the children have developed greater powers of discrimination, and a chart or map may be made by pasting colored squares, triangles, oblongs, or circles on a ground of gray Bristol board.

Then, too, we may have a box of tablets of the simple geometrical figures, and, giving a quantity to the children, let them arrange the different colors in separate rows.

Children of all ages will be fascinated by the spectrum, "Nature's palette of pure colors," which the sunlight streaming through a prism shows upon the wall; and as it can be supplemented by a spectrum chart for cloudy days, they will delight to arrange their colored papers to imitate it. The older children will gain much valuable knowledge by experimenting with the color tops, and if a color wheel with the accompanying Maxwell [Pg 22]disks can be obtained, the materials for color education will be quite complete.

It must not be forgotten that the purpose of all these exercises is that the child may learn to know the six standards, and subsequently their intermediates, and may in time learn to use and combine them harmoniously. It is, therefore, essential that the colors supplied him shall be fresh and pure,[15] and that he not only have freedom to make his own experiments, but materials to preserve them in permanent form when they prove successful.

When the children are just making friends with the teacher and with each other, it is very interesting and profitable for them to formulate their mite of knowledge into a sentence, each one holding his ball high in the air with the right hand, and saying:—

My ball is red like a cherry.
My ball is yellow like a lemon.
My ball is blue like the sky.
My ball is orange like a marigold.
My ball is green like the grass.
My ball is violet like a plum.

We should not, however, allow this to degenerate into mere recitation, but let the child find [Pg 23]his own objects of comparison, and change them when he chooses for any others that occur to him. This prevents parrot repetition, and gives room for individuality and real self-expression.

MOTION; DIRECTION; POSITION.

Motion; Direction; Position.

The child of three or four years has seldom any conception of the terms:—

Right ——
Left.
Here ——
There.

Up ——
Down.
Near ——
Far.

Over ——
Under.
Front —
— Back.

Even if he has a dim idea of direction, he cannot express himself regarding it, nor is he certain enough of his knowledge to be able to move or place the ball according to dictation.

Motion is always easy and delightful to the child, and therefore he will move his ball in different directions, as the words and music suggest, when he would be too timid to express a thought, and is willing and happy to do in unison what he would hesitate to do by himself.

The ball may be made a starting-point in giving the child an idea of various simple facts about objects in general, and in illustrating in movements the many terms with which we wish him to become familiar. The meaning of the terms to *swing, hop, jump, roll, spring, run away, come back, fall, draw, bounce,* and *push* may be taught by a like movement of the ball, urging the child to give his own interpretation of the [Pg 24]motions in words. All the children may then make their balls hop, spring, roll, or swing at the same time, accompanying the movements by appropriate rhymes.

The ball is more purely a plaything than anything which the child receives in the kindergarten, and its mobility is so charming, it so easily slips from his hands and travels so delightfully far when dropped, that exercises with it soon become riotous if not carefully guided. Every play-lesson on the ball should close with some active exercise in which the children may indulge their wish for a game with their dear playfellow, and in which they may also gain greater skill and learn practically the laws of motion.

When sitting at their tables, each pair of children may roll a ball to and fro, all beginning at the same moment; or the first pair may begin, the second and third follow, and so on until all are rolling. They may throw balls against the wall, or toss them in the air, or throw them alternately first in the air, then against the wall; they may toss them to each other at increasing distances. The whole company of children may be arranged in two rows and throw the balls to each other in unison, or they may pass them from hand to hand as in a Wandering Game,—all the exercises being accompanied with appropriate songs or rhymes.

The laws of incidence and reflection may be [Pg 25]simply taught by leading the children to note that if they strike the ball straight against the wall it will bound straight back, and then asking them to see if it returns when thrown in a slanting direction.

Symbolic Stage of Child's Development.

In order to present the ball in a more attractive light in the kindergarten, to suit it to the symbolic stage of the child's development, and to bring it nearer to his sympathies, we constantly, in our play, suppose it to be something which it resembles in certain of its characteristics. By its color, it may represent a fruit, a flower, or a gayly dressed child; by its form, an egg, a downy chicken, a tiny duckling; by its mobility, a bird, a squirrel, a baby; or when fastened to its string, a bucket in the well, a toy wagon, a pendulum, or a pet lamb tethered by the roadside.

The child is always at home in the world of "make-believe," and delights in the stories and the many charming songs to which this imaginative use of the ball gives rise.

Perhaps we may wisely remind ourselves, however, that though the child's fancy is most vivid, and though the ball is well adapted to represent many objects, yet if it resemble in no single point the thing to which we liken it, we are indulging in empty imaginings which will only hinder the child's comprehension of truth.[16]

Coöperative Exercises.

[Pg 26]The teacher who truly understands the great principles on which Froebel built the kindergarten will ever be mindful of one of the highest of these,—"the brotherly union of those who are like-minded." Even in the simple plays with the first gift, group work is easily possible. The stringing of the first gift beads or the supplementary modeling in clay may be made into a coöperative exercise, the work with the balls at the sand-table may have a similar aim, and many of the ball games are well fitted to unite the whole community of children, older and younger, in a common aim, a common purpose.[17]

What we should strive for.

We must remember that on a carefully prepared plan of procedure depends much of the value of any system of education; therefore we must decide, when the child comes under our tutelage, what we wish to accomplish and what shall be our method of accomplishing it; and yet as the first gift is not the last, as it is but the first link in a chain of related [Pg 27]objects, it is obvious that it must be chiefly useful as a starting-point. Each lesson should be carefully studied by the teacher, for the foundation is being laid for all future acquisition.

The kindergarten gifts are designed to lead to the mastery of material objects, but at the same time they are always connected with the child's experience and affection by being often transported into the region of fancy and feeling in a blending of realism and symbolism. Omitting everything which has reference to the moral and physical development, and speaking now only of that which is intellectual, what we should strive for at the beginning is that the child may acquire a habit of quick observation, with clear and precise expression; that in due time he may see not only quickly, but accurately; in short, that a slight degree of judgment may begin to attend his perceptions, so that he may know as well as observe. It is not enough to awaken the curiosity of a child, and to heap up in his memory a mass of good materials which will combine of themselves in due time, and which the brain when more highly developed will arrange in systematic groups; we should endeavor as far as possible to control the first impressions which sink unconsciously into a child's mind, but still more careful should we be in the selection of those later ones which we try to inculcate, and of the links which we wish to establish between such and such perceptions, sentiments, or actions.

[Pg 28]We should seek to develop, side by side with the perceptions, the faculty of judging and acting rightly.

To give a child very little to observe at a time, but to make him observe that little well and rightly, is the true way of forming and storing his mind.

The process of receiving an idea must be through sensation, attention, and perception, conception and judgment being later processes. The curiosity to know must be kept alive, for it is our greatest ally, and the imagination must be fed, for the child remembers only what interests him.

Recognizing what is to be accomplished, we say, then:—

a. The ball is one of the first means used in awakening and developing the dawning consciousness and growing faculties of the child.

b. The beginning must be well made, or no later step will seem clear.

c. If the first opportunity which occurs of dealing with the gift (or with any instrumentality of education) is wasted, interest on the part of the child is permanently lessened.

d. The mind retains clear impressions in proportion to the degree of spontaneous interest and attention with which they are received.

e. The law of diminishing interest decrees that each point in a successful exercise shall be more interesting than the previous one.

[Pg 29]*f.* The lessons must not be confined to so narrow a channel that they become monotonous, and they must leave room for the child to develop and not attempt to prescribe his mental action.

Tiedemann says: "Liberty of action even in imitated actions is one of the conditions of a child's happiness; besides that, it has the effect of exercising and developing all his faculties. Example is the first tutor, and liberty the second, in the order of evolution; but the second is the better one, for it has inclination for its assistant."

READINGS FOR THE STUDENT.

From Cradle to School. *Bertha Meyer.* Pages 118-20.
Education. *Herbert Spencer.* 128-40.
Kindergarten Culture. *W. N. Hailmann.* 41-46.
Education. *E. Seguin.* 7, 8.
The Kindergarten. *Emily Shirreff.* 10.
Kindergarten at Home. *Emily Shirreff.* 46.
Reminiscences of Froebel. *Von Marenholtz-Bülow.* 208, 209.
Lectures on Child-Culture. *W. N. Hailmann.* 24.
Kindergarten Guide. *J. and B. Ronge.* 1-3.
Koehler's Kindergarten Practice. Tr. by *Mary Gurney.* 5-12.
Child-Culture. *Henry Barnard.* 567, 568, 570-75.
Education of Man. *Fr. Froebel.* Tr. by *J. Jarvis.* 105, 106, 206.
Lectures to Kindergartners. *E. P. Peabody.* 30, 31, 38, 39, 44-51.
Pedagogics of the Kindergarten. *Fr. Froebel.* Tr. by *J. Jarvis.* 31-69.
Paradise of Childhood. *Edward Wiebe.* 7-9.
Law of Childhood. *W. N. Hailmann.* 31-33.
Kindergarten Guide. *Kraus-Boelte.* 1-15.
Froebel and Education by Self-Activity. *H. Courthope Bowen.* 136-38.
[Pg 30]Childhood's Poetry and Studies. *E. Marwedel.* Part I. 7-15.
Childhood's Poetry and Studies. *E. Marwedel.* Part II. 6-17.
A System of Child-Culture. *E. Marwedel.* 1-5.
The Dawn of History. *A. Keary.* 44-47.
Hints to Teachers. *E. Marwedel.* 5, 6.

Froebel's Letters. Tr. by *Michaelis* and *Moore*. 83-85, 98, 101-03, 107, 176, 220.

Conscious Motherhood. E. *Marwedel*. 106, 107, 118, 119, 153, 162-64, 170-74, 256-62, 291-96.

THE CUBE

[Pg 31]

FROEBEL'S SECOND GIFT

"From the ball as a symbol of unity, we pass over in a consecutive manner to the manifoldness of form in the cube."

"The child has an intimation in the cube of the unity which lies at the foundation of all manifoldness, and from which the latter proceeds."

FRIEDRICH FROEBEL.

"Notice has now become observation, and observation leads to discrimination. He sees and is curious by nature, but it belongs to us to lead him to observe and inquire."

EMILY SHIRREFF.

1. Froebel's second gift consists of a wooden sphere, cube, and cylinder, two inches in diameter (as now made), with rods and standards for revolution.[18]

2. In the first gift the child received objects of the same shape and size but of different colors, thus learning to separate color from form. In the second gift he receives unlike objects, and learns to distinguish them from each other by their individual peculiarities. The first gift suggests unity, and leads to the detection of resemblances; the second suggests variety or manifoldness, and emphasizes contrasts.

[Pg 32]3. The most important characteristic of the gift is contrast of form, leading to the distinction of different objects. The mediation of contrasts here suggests the connection of all objects, however widely separated.

4. The purpose of the gift is to stimulate observation and comparison by presentation of striking contrasts, and to afford new bases for the classification of objects. Spencer says that any systematic ministrations to the perceptions ought to be based upon the general truth that in the development of every faculty markedly contrasted impressions are the first to be distinguished; that hence sounds greatly differing in loudness and pitch, colors very remote from each other, and substances widely removed in hardness or texture should be the first supplied; and that in each case the progression must be by slow degrees to impressions more nearly allied.[19]

5. The geometrical forms illustrated in this gift are:—

```
              {
      Sphere.

              { Cube.
    ʂ         {
 olids.  Cylinder.

              {                  } Seen in
      Double Cone.     motion.
              {                  }
      Conoid.


    I         {
 lanes.  Circles.
              {
      Squares.
```

6. The sphere and cube are sharply contrasting [Pg 33]forms, and the cylinder illustrates the connecting link between the two, possessing characteristics of both.

"The cylinder is the first example Froebel gives of the intermediate transition—forms connecting opposites, which he explains as the very ground plan of Nature, and on which his fundamental law of contrasts and connection of contrasts, the law of all harmonious development and creative industry, is based."[20]

Points to be noted in each New Gift.

"That which follows is always conditioned upon that which goes before,"[21] says Froebel, and he makes this apparent to children through his educational processes; the gifts show this idea in concrete form.

In entering upon a consideration of the second gift one thing cannot fail to impress us, and that is the continuous development in each new set of objects placed before the child; together with an increase of difficulty or complexity which is never without a corresponding forethought, careful arrangement, and attention to logical sequence; thus the newly introduced objects can never seem unnatural to him.

We shall find that in every new gift or occupation there is always a suggestion of the last, [Pg 34]enough to make it a pleasant reminder of knowledge gained and difficulties surmounted, and so the child sees not everything painfully strange, but something which at least recalls to his mind his former friend and familiar playfellow.[22]

Method of Attack in First Exercise.

In the first lesson with the second gift the child will quickly see the similarities between his former worsted ball and his new companion, the wooden sphere. Let him take these two balls together, and find out the similarities and dissimilarities, remembering that before he compares objects *consciously*, experiences should invariably be given him.

We should always draw attention to the universal properties of things first and then proceed to the specific. The qualities common to all objects are the universal ones: Form, Size, Color, Material, etc. The invariable rule should be: simple before complex, concrete before abstract, unity before variety, universal qualities before special ones.

If we are in doubt as to whether we shall first direct attention to the similarities or to the dissimilarities between the ball and sphere, we may recall the educational maxim, "The child's eye [Pg 35]always at first seizes the analogous, the point of union, the whole connection of things, and only after that begins to discern differences and opposition."[23]

Ball and Sphere.

In comparing the ball and the sphere the child will observe, in the first place that they are both round and both roll equally well, but that one has color, one being without; one is soft, the other hard; one quiet, one noisy; one a little rough to the touch, the other velvet smooth. He should find for and by himself, aided by our suggestive questioning, the reasons for these evident differences.

It is absolutely necessary that each child should have one of the boxes containing the solids, or at least the three forms of the gift without the box, rods, and standards, and examine them thoroughly and often as he will be glad to do.

If the solids as ordinarily manufactured are too costly for a kindergartner of limited means, she can substitute large marbles, blocks, and linen thread spools; the material does not matter so long as each child has the objects to handle.

Value of the Discriminative Power; Method by which it may be developed.

We need not be distressed if the lessons are a little noisy when the children are making the acquaintance of these wonderful new friends. To be sure they will pound the wooden forms heartily up and down on the table (if they are [Pg 36]three-year old babies, they certainly would and should do so); but within bounds what does it matter? If it can be arranged so that other classes shall not be disturbed, and each child can have the same opportunity for experimenting as his neighbor, there will be no great harm done.

We are endeavoring to rouse all the latent energies of the child by the presentation of these objects to his observation, and he must have full liberty to make the various experiments which suggest themselves to him. His desire to hear the sound of the objects is so manifest that it would be folly to try and thwart it. It is far better to use the desire for educational purposes and divert it into the channel of systematized noise. Let us suppose that we are carpenters today and pound the wooden objects on the floor in exact time with a building song; let us play we are drummer boys and tap with our drumsticks for the soldiers to march; or shall we make believe that the sphere is a woodpecker and let it tap on the trees while we recite some simple little rhyme?[24]

"This craving of young children for information," says Bernard Perez, "is an emotional and intellectual absorbing power, as dominant as the appetite for nutrition, and equally needing to be watched over and regulated."

[Pg 37]It is not alone the noise of the sphere which delights the child,[25] though this is always pleasing,—it is the knowledge he is gaining, the new ideas that dawn upon him for the first time in recognizable form. It is, in fact, a knowledge of cause and effect. He has often dropped the woolen ball and pounded it on the table, and it produced no sound. He does the same with the sphere and recognizes the difference. He will begin to experiment with other objects, by and by to classify his knowledge, and finally, he will see and remember that like causes produce like effects, and in progressing thus far will have made a tremendous stride. The child will see all the more clearly, in comparing the woolen ball and wooden sphere, the difference between soft and hard, rough and smooth, light and heavy, if he is allowed to perform his own experiments.

The Cube.

We will now turn to the investigation of the cube and open a new world of information to the child, and here we seem to deviate a little from the famous educational maxim, "Proceed from the known to the unknown," and almost to make a leap into the dark. However, we very soon give the cylinder, and thus connect the opposites. Here he meets a dazzling [Pg 38]quantity of new appearances; the square sides or faces, and the many edges and corners, all of which must be viewed in comparison with the sphere. We can give him an experience of the faces of the cube without conscious analysis, by letting the ball roll against them.

Mediation of Contrasts.

Of course we shall see the underlying idea of the gift to be the connection of opposites. Not too much can be said of this law, so all-important and significant in Froebel's system.[26] We should bear it constantly in mind, and bring it in connection with every new phase of our work. Froebel cannot be understood clearly unless this deep principle, which lies at the very root of his system, is appreciated and comprehended. At the same time it is, when formulated, an abstract and metaphysical statement, which one cannot grasp at once, but to which one must grow.

It may be said that comparatively few kindergartners know its value; nevertheless knowledge of this kind can never be useless or fruitless to the person who is forming the mind of the child, and who should be a perfect mistress of her science and her art.

Value of Contrasts.

[Pg 39]These contrasts of the second gift, and all contrasts, arouse the mind to attention. We can have no judgment without comparison. We should have no idea of heat or darkness if we had not a conception of cold and light; the quality of sweetness would have no meaning if its opposite did not serve to stimulate comparison.

The sphere is sharply contrasted with the cube, so that there may be a ready perception of the striking qualities of both. The more abrupt the contrast the more readily noticed and described; for it takes a more developed eye to discern the difference between a sphere and a spheroid, for instance, than between a sphere and a cube.

The contrasts of the first gift were contrasts of color, mediations of them being shown also, and contrasts of direction and position or situation. Another point less readily seen in the first gift perhaps was Froebel's thought that the ball, in its perfect simplicity and unity, when first given to the young child, is regarded by him as another contrasted individuality, almost as capable of life in its varied movements as he is himself.

Mobility of Sphere.

The sphere is the symbol of motion, the cube the embodiment of rest, and the fact should be illustrated in divers ways. We may, for instance, place the sphere near the [Pg 40]rim of a plate, and by inclining the latter a little, the sphere will roll rapidly round its own axis and round the rim. A few simple little rhymes may be taught, which the children may say or sing together while the sphere is journeying rapidly round and round the plate, for, as Froebel says, the thought always grows clearer to the child when word and motion go hand in hand.

Sphere and Cube.

The cube can only be moved, on the contrary, when force is exerted, and then it merely slides, to stop when the force is removed. The children will soon see why the cube is so lazily inclined, and why the sphere is ever rolling, rolling about, scarcely to be kept still, for by various experiments we may show that the sphere stands only on a little part of its face, the cube on the whole.

The sphere is always the same in whatever way regarded, and to whatever tests subjected. It is always an emblem of unity, and cannot be robbed of its simplicity, its unity, its freedom from all that is puzzling.

The cube, on the contrary, being made to revolve on any one of its axes, constantly shows a different aspect, so that the child views it as a very extraordinary little block, full of fascinating surprises and whimsical apparitions.

It is put upon the string, and, when whirled rapidly, mysteriously loses its identity, and appears to the little one's laughing gaze as an [Pg 41]entirely different object; and yet as the motion grows more sedate, the new form fades away and the cube reappears so quickly as to make him rub his eyes and wonder if he has been dreaming.

Counting Faces.

The square faces of the cube, in comparison with the one curved, unbroken surface of the sphere, must now be noted, and may be counted if we are using the gift as a means of instruction.

We must beware, however, of making this counting exercise into a lesson, or requiring that the number of faces shall be learned and recited. Every teacher of experience will corroborate Mr. W. N. Hailmann when he says: "If the kindergartner sets the cube before the child and counts the faces, edges, and corners, so that he may 'know all about it,' the child's interest, if born at all, will soon die."

If the faces are counted, as they are all so exactly alike, the children may sometimes be puzzled as to the number, by enumerating the same one more than once. This difficulty may be obviated by pasting a paper square of a different color on each face, and then submitting it to examination, giving each child an opportunity to count, since independent self-activity is to be more and more encouraged.

If the faces, edges, and corners be made the integral point of an interesting story or play, the child will have little difficulty in recalling their [Pg 42]number and character, but we must remember that "lively interest and steady progress come only from following and feeding the child's purposes."

Cylinder.

We now proceed to the cylinder, the reconciliation of the two opposites; an object which having qualities possessed by both occupies a middle ground in which each has something in common.

Froebel originally took the doll[27] as the intermediate form "uniting in itself the opposites of the sphere and cube," and thus showed that he understood child nature well, for no toy follows the ball with greater certainty than the doll.

The cylinder, however, was subsequently selected, as being more in line with the other geometrical forms shown in the sequence of gifts. It is as easily moved as the sphere, upon one side; as prone to rest as the cube, when placed upon the other; it has the curved surface of the sphere and the flat faces of the cube; it has no corners but two curved edges; more edges than the sphere, fewer than the cube; less unity than the sphere, more than the cube.

Its importance as a mediation, or connecting [Pg 43]link, is further shown by suspending the cube on a string, by which it may be twisted rapidly and caused to revolve; in this motion a cylinder being readily seen. When the cylinder is spun in like manner a sphere suddenly appears, and so the wonderful and subtle bond of union is complete.[28]

Hints as to Manner and Method.

Let the children call the cylinder a "roller" or "barrel" if they choose, and tell them the right name when it is needful. Each gift must be thoroughly understood before we pass to the next, or there will be no orderly development; but as the impressions have all been made through the senses of the child, we must not expect him to voice these impressions in logical phrases all at once, so beware of making the lesson irksome or wearisome to him through a formal questioning that does not properly belong to childhood.

When the keen appetite for knowledge disappears we may well despair. If several children in our class express dislike of a certain exercise or lesson, and seem to dread its appearance, we may be well assured that the fault lies in our method [Pg 44]of putting it before them, and strive in all humility for a better understanding of them, of ourselves, and of the subject.

We must not, however, be too hard in our self-judgments and lose courage. We are not responsible for a child who is "born tired," and who seems to have no interest in anything, either in heaven above or in the earth beneath, until, by ingenuity and perseverance, we are able to open the eyes and ears which see and hear not.

It will be remembered that in discussing the first play or lesson with the second gift great freedom was advised; but let us note the difference between liberty and lawlessness, between spontaneity and the confusion of self-assertion which is sometimes mistaken for it.

No lesson or play amounts to anything unless conducted with order and harmony, unless at its close, no matter how merry and hearty the enjoyment, some quiet and lasting impression has been made on the mind. Many teachers miss the happy medium, and in trying with the best intentions to allow the individuality of the child proper development, only succeed in gaining excitement and disorder.

Dangers of Object Lessons.

The second gift is, more than any other, too much used for mere object lessons, and these are invariably dangerous because there is apt to be too much impressing of the teacher's own ideas upon the mind, and too little [Pg 45]actual handling, perceiving, observing, comparing, judging, concluding, on the child's part, and that is the only logical way in which he is able to form a clearly crystallized idea.

We can have no higher authority than Dr. Alexander Bain, who says that the object lesson more than anything else demands a careful handling; there being "great danger lest an admirable device should settle down into a plausible but vicious formality."

How to deal successfully with Second Gift.

It is not uncommon to hear students in kindergarten training classes (and even some full-fledged kindergartners) express a distaste for the second gift, and it is, unfortunately, even more common to find the children dealing with it either sunk in deepest apathy, or mercifully oblivious of the matter in hand and chatting with their neighbors. The fact is that we have too commonly made the exercises dull, dreary affairs; we have doled out the forms to the children and asked a series of formal questions about them, giving no experiments, no concerted work, and no opportunity for action. The children have been intensely bored, therefore either stupid or wandering, and the kindergartner has attributed her want of success to the gift, and not to her method of dealing with it.

Let the light of imagination shine on the scene, and note the answering sparkle in the children's [Pg 46]eyes. Who cares for the names of all the faces on a stupid block; but who doesn't care when it's a house and Johnnie can't find his mother, though he looks in the front door and the back door, the right-hand door, the left-hand door, the cellar-door, and finally the trap-door leading to the roof? Nobody knows, or wants to know, when questioned if the cylinder rolls better on its flat circular face, or on its rounding face; but when it's a log of wood in the forest, and must be taken home for winter fires, then it is worth while to experiment and see how it may be moved most easily.

The second gift, too, is delightful for groupwork in the sand table, where the objects may be treated symbolically, and likened to a hundred different things. With the second gift beads, which in the natural wood color are admirable supplements to the larger forms, the children are always charmed, assorting and stringing them according to fancy or dictation, and with the addition of sticks making them into rows of soldiers, trees in flowerpots, kitchen utensils, churns, stoves, lamps, and divers other household objects.

The kindergartner may give many a lesson in the simple principles of mechanics with the second gift and its rods and standards, allowing the children to experiment freely as well as to follow her suggestions. The pulley, the steelyard, [Pg 47]the capstan, the pump, the mechanical churn, the wheelbarrow, etc., may all be made, adding the beads where necessary, and thus the child gain a real working knowledge of simple machinery.

Treatment of Previous Gifts when passed over.

The preceding gift need not entirely disappear, but be used occasionally for a pleasing review as a bond of friendly intercourse between older and younger pupils.[29] This will convey an indirect hint, perhaps, to the little ones that it is not well to neglect old friends for new ones, but that they should still love and value the playthings and playmates of former days.

Second Gift Forms in Architecture and Cube in Ancient Times.

These three objects, the sphere, cylinder, and cube, constitute a triad of forms united in architecture and sculpture producing the column, which is made up of the pedestal or base (the cube), the shaft (the cylinder), and the capital (the sphere).

In a book on Egyptian antiquities we find that, in the beginning of the culture of that country, the three Graces, or goddesses of beauty, were represented by three cubes leaning upon each other. The Egyptians did not, of course, know that it was the first regular form of solid bodies in [Pg 48]nature or crystallization; but the significant fact again brings us to the thought expressed in the first lecture: "It would seem, indeed, as though Froebel, in selecting his gifts, looked far back into the past of humanity, and there sought the thread which from the beginning connects all times and leads to the farthest future."

Froebel's Monument.

And here we leave the second gift, that trinity of forms which, wrought in marble, marks the place dear and sacred to all kindergartners, the grave of Froebel,—a simple monument to one so great, yet so connected with our study and the child's experience that with all its simplicity it is strangely effective. A still more enduring monument he has in the millions of happy children who have found their way to knowledge through the door which he opened to them; indeed, if half the children he has benefited could build a tower of these tiny blocks to commemorate his life and death, its point would reach higher than St. Peter's dome and draw the thoughts of men to heaven.

Suggestions of the Gift.

This gift can hardly be studied but that an inner unity, born of these reconciled contrasts, suggests itself to the imagination.

The cube seems to stand as the symbol of the inorganic, the mineral kingdom, with its wonderful crystals; the cylinder as the type of vegetable life, suggesting the roots, stems, and branches, [Pg 49]with their rounded sides, and forming a beautiful connection between the cube, that emblem of "things in the earth beneath," and the sphere which completes the trinity and speaks to us of a never-ending and perfect whole having "Unity for its centre, Diversity for its circumference."

The cube seems to suggest rest, immobility; the cylinder, in this connection, growth; and the sphere, perfection, completeness,—so delicately poised it is,—only kept in its proper place by the most exquisite adjustment. And so to us, sometimes, the things that are visible become luminous with suggestions of greater realities which are yet unseen; and in the least we discern a faint radiance of the greatest.

Things that are small mirror things that are mighty. The tiny sphere is an emblem of the "big round world" and the planetary systems. The cube recalls the wonderful crystals, and shows the form that men reflect in architecture and sculpture. As for the cylinder it is Nature's special form, and God has taught man through Nature to use it in a thousand ways, and indeed has himself fashioned man more or less in its shape.

Mr. Hailmann says: "The second gift presents types of the principal phases of human development; from the easy mobility of infancy and childhood,—the ball,—we pass through the [Pg 50]half-steady stages of boyhood and girlhood, represented in the cylinder, to the firm character of manhood and womanhood for which the cube furnishes the formula."

Bishop Brooks, speaking from the words, "The length and the breadth of it are equal," in his sermon on Symmetry of Life, uses the cube as a symbol of perfect character: The personal push of a life forward, its outreach laterally or the going out in sympathy to others, the upward reach toward God,—these he considers the three life dimensions. But such building must be done without nervous haste; the foundation must hint solidly of the threefold purpose; length, breadth, and thickness must be kept in proportion, if the perfect cube of life is ever to be found.

NOTE ON SECOND GIFT.[30] "The second gift, even in the nursery, calls for modifications from the form in which it comes to us from Froebel. It is incomparable in its rich symbolism for illustrating Froebel's thought to mature minds, and answers quite a useful purpose in the nursery, where it may help mamma tell her stories. But in the kindergarten the child wants to build with blocks. Hence, the third, fourth, fifth, and sixth gifts are indicated; the second gift, as such, is, to say the least, an anachronism. Only in the form of the beads, or some similar expedient [Pg 51]which gives many of these things for control, will it satisfy the kindergarten child. When he is expected to *study* the cube, as an object lesson, to count the squares and corners and tell where they are, it is wholly unpalatable to him and entirely foreign to his plans."

THOUGHTS ON THE DISCRIMINATIVE POWER.

"Mind starts from Discrimination. The consciousness of difference is the beginning of every intellectual exercise."

"Our intelligence is, therefore, absolutely limited by our power of discrimination; the other functions of intellect, the retentive power, for instance, are not called into play until we have first discriminated a number of things."

"The minuteness or delicacy of the feeling of difference is the measure of the variety and multitude of our primary impressions and therefore of our stored-up recollections."

"Bear in mind the fact that until a difference is felt between two things, intelligence has not yet made the first step."

"The higher arts of comparison to impress difference are best illustrated when both differences and agreements have to be noted, i. e., similarities and dissimilarities."

"Discrimination is the necessary prelude of[Pg 52] every intellectual impression as the basis of our stored-up knowledge or memory."

Definition of the state of mind significantly named *Indifference*,—"the state where differing impressions fail to be recognized as distinct."

"The retentive power works up to the height of the discriminative power; it can do no more."

ALEX. BAIN.

"The most delightful and fruitful of all the intellectual energies is the perception of similarity and agreement, by which we rise from the individual to the general, trace sameness in diversity, and master instead of being mastered by the multiplicity of nature."

FRIEDRICH FROEBEL.

"It is by comparisons that we ascertain the difference which exists between things, and it is by comparisons, also, that we ascertain the general features of things, and it is by comparisons that we reach general propositions. In fact, comparisons are at the bottom of all philosophy."

LOUIS AGASSIZ.

READINGS FOR THE STUDENT.

From Cradle to School. *Bertha Meyer.* Pages 132, 133.
The Kindergarten. *Emily Shirreff.* 11, 12.
Lectures on Child-Culture. *W. N. Hailmann.* 26, 27.
Froebel and Education by Self-Activity. *H. Courthope Bowen.* 138-40.

Kindergarten Guide. *J.* and *B. Ronge.* 3-5.
Koehler's Kindergarten Practice. Tr. by *Mary Gurney.* 47-49.
[Pg 53]
Kindergarten at Home. *Emily Shirreff.* 47-49.
Kindergarten Culture. *W. N. Hailmann.* 46, 51, 54.
Childhood's Poetry and Studies. *E. Marwedel.* Part II. 16-42.
Pedagogics of the Kindergarten. *Fr. Froebel.* 69-107.
Paradise of Childhood. *Edward Wiebe.* 9-11.
Law of Childhood. *W. N. Hailmann.* 33-35.
Kindergarten Guide. *Kraus-Boelte.* 15-27.
Education of Man. *Fr. Froebel.* 107-10.
Kindergarten Toys. *H. Hoffmann.* 12-17.
Architecture, Mysticism, and Myth. *W. K. Lethaby.* 50, 65.
Stories of Industry. Vols. i. and ii. *A. Chase* and *E. Clow.*
Ethics of the Dust. *John Ruskin.*
Mme. A. de Portugall's Synoptical Table, as given in "Essays on the Kindergarten."

[Pg 54]

THE BUILDING GIFTS

The Building Gifts meet two very strongly marked tendencies in the child. *a.* The tendency to investigate. *b.* The tendency to transform.

The first and second gifts consist of undivided units, each one of which stands in relation to a larger whole, or to a class of objects.

The third, fourth, fifth, and sixth gifts are divided units, and their significance lies in the relationship of the parts to one another, and to the whole of which they are the parts.

The effect of the Building Gifts is to develop the constructive powers of the child. Their secondary importance lies in the fact that they afford striking fundamental perceptions of Form, Size, Number, Relation, and Position.

The following rules should govern the dictation exercises:—

BUILDING RULES.

1. Use all material in order to keep the idea of relation of parts to a whole, and because all unused material is wasted material.[31]

[Pg 55]2. Build on the squares of the table in order to develop accuracy and symmetry.

3. "Induce the child to form other wholes gradually and systematically from the various parts of the cube. In doing this the laws of contrast and development must be your guide."

KOEHLER.

4. Give names to each object constructed, thereby bringing it into relation with the child's experience; for the miniature model serves to interpret more clearly to him the object which it represents.

5. Connect with the child's life and sympathy in order to increase his interest and develop the tendency to view things in their right relations.

6. "The younger the child, the more you should talk about the thing which you intend to construct. You should intersperse passing observations or short songs. As the children gain intelligence, this conversation will be replaced by more formal descriptions of the things represented."

KOEHLER.

7. Begin with Life forms and proceed from these to forms of Beauty and Knowledge.

8. Allow no child to rely upon the blocks of his playmates in his building,—thus he will learn economy, self-reliance, and independence of action. [Pg 56]This should not be carried too far, or rather the necessity and beauty of interdependence should also be taught. Herein, indeed, lies more than at first appears. To make the most out of little is the great work of life; to be contented with what one has, and to make the best of it with happiness and contentment is surely no small lesson, and one which is constantly, though indirectly, taught in the kindergarten work and plays and lessons.

9. Group work, or united building, should frequently be introduced. "Every direction given by the kindergartner should be followed by spontaneous work (either in word or deed) by the child. This must not only be individual, but synthesized for the community."

10. Often encourage the class to imitate some specially attractive form which has been produced by a child, and named according to his fancy.

11. Accustom the child to develop figures or forms by slight changes rather than by rudely destroying each single one preparatory to constructing another. From learning to be strictly methodical in his actions, he will become so in his later reasoning.

12. "Let the child, if possible, correct his own mistakes, and do not constantly interfere with his work. Whatever he is able to do for himself, no one should do for him."

KOEHLER.

[Pg 57]
FROEBEL'S THIRD GIFT

"All children have the building instinct, and 'to make a house' is a universal form of unguided play."

"It is not a mere pastime, but a key with which to open the outer world, and a means of awakening the inner world."

"This gift includes in itself more outward manifoldness, and, at the same time, makes the inward manifoldness yet more perceptible and manifest."

"The plaything shows also the ultimate type of structures put together by human hand which stand in their substantiality around the child."

FRIEDRICH FROEBEL.

"The definitely productive exercises begin with the third gift."

SUSAN E. BLOW.

1. The third gift is a wooden cube measuring two inches in each of its dimensions. It is divided once in its height, breadth, and thickness, according to the three dimensions which define a solid, and thus eight smaller cubes are produced.

2. We pass from the undivided to the divided unit, emphasizing the fact that unity still exists, though divisibility enters as a new factor.

3. The most important characteristics of the gift are contrasts of size resulting in the abstraction of form from size; increase of material as a whole, decrease of size in parts; increase of facilities in illustrating form and number.

[Pg 58]The new experience to be found in this first divided body is the idea of relativity; of the whole in its relation to the parts (each an embryo whole), and of the parts in relation to the whole.

The form of the parts is like the form of the whole, but, in shape alike, the dissimilarity is in size; the fact becoming more apparent by a variety of combinations of a different number of parts: thus the relations of numbers are introduced to the observation of the child together with those of form and magnitude.

4. The third gift was intended by Froebel to meet the necessities of the child at a period when, no longer satisfied with the external appearances of things, he strives to penetrate their internal conditions, and begins to realize the many different possibilities of the same element.

5. The geometrical forms illustrated in this gift are:—

S
olids.
{ Cube.
{ Square Prism.
{ Rectangular Parallelopiped.

P
lanes.
{ Square.
{ Oblong.

6. Froebel intends the building exercise to be carried on in a certain way with a view of establishing a law to regulate the child's activity. The upper and lower parts of the figure—the contrasts—are first brought into position, and [Pg 59]the balance is established by the intermediates—right and left.

The cube itself is divided according to the law of Mediation of Contrasts. The contrasts of exterior and interior, whole and parts, analysis and synthesis, are also brought into relation with each other.

Hailmann on Third Gift.

Mr. W. N. Hailmann says that the third gift marks an important step in the mental life of the child. Heretofore, he has had to do with playthings indivisible, whole, complete in themselves. Every impression, or, rather, every fact, came to him as a unit, a one, an indivisible whole.

The analyses and syntheses that are presented to him in the first and second gifts come ready-made as it were, so that the joyous exercise of his instinctive activity, guided and directed by the judicious, loving mother, is sufficient to give him control of them; indeed, the first and second gifts hold to his mental development the same relation that the mother's milk holds to his physical growth.

But the third gift satisfies the growing desire for independent activity, for the exercise of his own power of analysis and synthesis, of taking apart and putting together.[32]

Simplicity but Adaptability of the Gifts.

[Pg 60]Simple as this first building gift appears, it is capable of great things. It lends itself to a hundred practical lessons and a hundred charming transformations, but if it is not thoroughly comprehended it will never be well or effectively used by the kindergartner, and will be nothing more to her than to uninterested observers, who see in it nothing more than eight commonplace little blocks in a wooden box.

Froebel says if his educational materials are found useful it cannot be because of their exterior, which is as plain as possible and contains nothing new, but that their worth is to be found exclusively in their application.

How Children are to be reached.

Therefore these simple devices with which we carry on our education should never seem trifling, for we are compelled in teaching very young children to put forth all gentle allurements to the gaining of knowledge.

They are to be reached chiefly by the charms of sense, novelty, and variety, and consequently, to please such active and imaginative little critics, our lessons must be fresh, vivid, vigorous, and to the point.

What is Necessary on Part of Kindergartner.

To accomplish this, we can see that not only is absolute knowledge necessary, but that a well developed sensibility and imagination are needed [Pg 61]in leading the child from the indefinite to the definite, from universal to particular, and from concrete to abstract. The worth of the gifts then, we repeat, lies exclusively in their application; the rude little forms must be used so that the child's imagination and sympathy will be reached.

Imagination in Child and Kindergartner.

We may be thankful that this heaven-born imaginative faculty is the heritage of every child,—that it is hard to kill and lives on very short rations. The little boy ties a string around a stone and drags it through dust and mire with happy conviction that it is a go-cart. The little girl wraps up a stocking or a towel with tender hands, winds her shawl about it, and at once the God-given maternal instinct leaps into life,—in an instant she has it in her arms. She kisses its cotton head and sings it to sleep in divine unconsciousness of any incompleteness, for love supplies many deficiencies. So let us cherish the child heart in ourselves and never look with scorn upon the rude suggestions of the forms the child has built, but rather enter into the play, enriching it with our own imaginative power. The children will rarely perceive any incongruities, and surely we need not hint them, any more than we would remind a child needlessly that her doll is stuffed with sawdust and has a plaster head, when she thinks it a responsive and affectionate little daughter.

[Pg 62]Middendorf said, "This is like a fresh bath for the human soul, when we dare to be children again with children.[33] The burdens of life could not be borne were it not for real gayety of heart."

"If it were only the play and the mere outward apparatus," says the Baroness von Marenholtz-Bülow, "we might indeed find our daily teaching monotonous, but the idea at the foundation of it and the contemplation of the being of man and its development in the child is an inexhaustible mine of interesting discovery."

Reasons for Choice of Third Gift.

This third gift satisfies the child's craving to take things to pieces. Froebel did not choose it arbitrarily, for Nature, human and physical, was an open handbook to him, and if we study deeply and sympathetically the reasons for his choice they will always be comprehended.[34] Fénelon says, "The curiosity of children is a natural tendency, which goes in the van of instruction." Destruction after all is only [Pg 63]constructive faculty turned back upon itself. The child, having no legitimate outlet for his creative instinct, pulls his playthings to pieces, to see what is inside,—what they are made of and how they are put together;[35] but to his chagrin he finds it not so easy to reunite the tattered fragments.

In the divided cube, however, he can gratify his desires, and at the same time possess the joy of doing right and destroying nothing, for the eight little blocks can be quickly united into their original form, and also into many other pleasing little forms, each one complete in itself, so that every analysis ends as it should, in synthesis.

Froebel calls this gift specifically "the children's delight," and indeed it is, responding so generously to their spontaneous activity, while at the same time it suits their small capabilities, for the possibilities of an object used for form study should not be too varied. "It must be suggestive through its limitations," says Miss Blow, "for the young mind may be as easily crushed by excess as by defect."[36]

[Pg 64]Froebel was left motherless at a very early age, and during his first four years of life his father was entirely engrossed with parish duties, and the child had only occasional supervision from a hard-worked servant. Thus it happened that he was frequently alone long hours at a time in a dusky room overshadowed by the neighboring church, and naturally strayed often to the window, from whence he might look down upon the busy world outside. He recalls that he was greatly interested at one time in some workmen who were repairing the church, and that he constantly turned from his post of observation to try and imitate their labors, but his only building material was the furniture of the room, and chairs and tables clumsily resisted his efforts to pile them up into suitable form. He tells us that this strong desire for building and the bitter disappointment of his repeated failures were still keenly remembered when he was a grown man, and thus suggested to him that children ought to be provided with materials for building among their playthings. He often noticed also, in later years, that all children seem to have the building instinct, corresponding to what Dr. Seguin calls "the building [Pg 65]mania in the infancy of peoples," and that "to make a house is the universal form of unguided play."[37]

We now understand the meaning of the gift, the reason for its importance in Froebel's plan, and its capabilities as a vehicle for delightful instruction.

Classes of Forms.

There are three different classes of forms for dictation and invention, variously named by kindergartners.

1. Life forms, or upright forms, which are seen in the child's daily life, as a pair of boots, a chair, table, bed, or sofa. Froebel calls them also object forms, or forms of things.

("The child demands that the object constructed stand in connection with himself, his life, or somebody or something in his life."—Froebel.)

2. Mathematical forms, or various combinations of the blocks, upright and supine, for mathematical exercises. They correspond to the forms of knowledge in Logic.

(Also called by Froebel forms of truth, forms of instruction, forms of learning.)

[Pg 66]3. Symmetrical forms, or flat designs formed by opposites and their intermediates. These are figures in which four of the blocks generally revolve in order around the other four as a centre.

(Also called by Froebel picture forms, flower forms, star forms, dance forms.)

LIFE FORMS.

Life Forms.

Life forms should be given first, as the natural tendency of the young child is to pile things up,[38]and these forms seem simpler for dictation, are more readily grasped by the mind, and more fascinating to the imagination. They are the images of things both dear and familiar to him, and thus are particularly adapted to the beginning since the "starting point of the child's development is the heart and the emotions." It is easier for him to be an architect at first than an artist, though each will be comprehended in the other after a time.[39]

[Pg 67]The dictations should be given very simply, clearly, and slowly, always using one set of terms to express a certain meaning, and having those absolutely correct. We should never give dictations from a book, but from memory, having prepared the lesson beforehand, and should remember that every exercise we give should "incite and develop self-activity." We must guard against mistakes or confusion in our own minds; it is very easy to confuse the child, and he will become inattentive and careless if he is unable to catch our meaning.

Brief stories should occasionally be told, just mere outlines to give color and force to the child's building, and connect it with his experience. If it is an armchair, grandmother may sit in it knitting the baby's stocking. If it is a well, describe the digging of it, the lining with stones or brick, the inflowing of the water, the letting down of the bucket and long chain, the clear, cool water coming up from the deep, dark hole in the ground on a hot summer's day. These, of course, are but the merest suggestions which experience may be trusted to develop.

It is better, perhaps, to give a bit of word-painting to each object constructed than to wait till the end of the series for the day and tell a [Pg 68]longer story, as the interest is thus more easily sustained. The children, too, should be encouraged to talk about the forms and tell little stories concerning them. The form created should never be destroyed, but transformed into the next in order by a few simple movements.

SYMMETRICAL FORMS.

Symmetrical Forms.

"These forms, in spite of their regularity, are called forms of beauty. The mathematical forms which Froebel designates forms of knowledge give only the skeleton from which the beautiful form develops itself.

"Symmetry of the parts which make up these simple figures gives the impression of beauty to the childish eye. He must have the elements of the beautiful before he is in a condition to comprehend it in its whole extent.

"Only what is simple gives light to the child at first. He can only operate with a small number of materials, therefore Froebel gives only eight cubes for this object at this time."

Of course these three classes of forms are not to be kept arbitrarily separate, and the children finish and lay aside one set before attempting another. There are many cases where the three may be united, as indeed they are morally speaking in the life of every human being.

When the distinctions are clear in our own minds, our knowledge and tact will guide us to [Pg 69]introduce the gift properly, and carry it on in a natural, orderly, and rational manner, not restricting the child's own productive powers.

If the children have had time to imbibe a love of symmetry and beauty, and have been trained to observe and delight in them, then this second class of forms will attract them as much, after a little, as the first, though more difficult of execution.

Each sequence starts from a definite point, the four outside blocks revolving round the central four, and going through or "dancing through," as Froebel says, all the successive figures before returning in the opposite direction.

All the dictations are most valuable intellectually, but should not be long-continued at one time, as they require great concentration of mind, and are consequently wearisome.

Hints from Ronge's "Guide."

Excellent exercises or suggestions for building can be found in Ronge's "Kindergarten Guide." He mentions one pleasant little play which I will quote. "When each in the class has produced a different form, let the children rise and march round the table to observe the variety." Let them sing in the ascending and descending scales:—

Many pretty forms I see,Which one seems the best to me?

At another time let each child try to build the [Pg 70]house he lives in, and while this is being done, let them join in singing some song about home. It is well to encourage singing during the building exercises, as we have so many appropriate selections.[40]

Group Work.

With the first of the Building Gifts enters a new variety of group work, which was not adapted for the first and second gifts. The children may now be seated at square tables, one at each side, and build in unison in the centre, the form produced being of course four times as large and fine as any one of the number could have produced alone. All the suggestions or directions for building are necessarily carried out together, and the success of the completed form is obviously dependent on the coöperation of all four children. Forms of Beauty are very easily constructed in this manner, as well as forms of Life, having four uniform sides, and when the little ones are somewhat more expert builders, Life forms having opposite sides alike, or even four different sides, may be constructed.

The other various forms of coöperative work are of course never to be neglected, that a social unity may be produced, in which "the might of each individual may be reinforced by the might of the whole."

[Pg 71]

MATHEMATICAL FORMS.

Mathematical Forms.

A better idea of these may be obtained through a manipulation of the blocks and an arrangement of the geometrical forms in their regular order.

The child, if he were taught as Froebel intended, would make his first acquaintance with numbers in the nursery, beginning in a very small way and progressing slowly. The pupils of the kindergarten are a little older, and having already a slight knowledge of numbers (though not of course in their abstract relations) are able to accomplish greater things.

The child can, with our guidance, make all possible combinations of the parts of the number Eight. The principles of Addition, Subtraction, even Multiplication and Fractions, can also be mastered without one tear of misery or pang of torture. He grasps the whole first, then by simple processes, building with his own hands, he finds out and demonstrates for himself halves, fourths, and eighths, sometimes in different positions, but always having the same contents.

Method and Manner of using the Gift.

Even yet we must not suffer this to become work. The exercises should be repeated again and again, but we must learn to break off when the play is still delightful, and study ways to endow the next one with new life and charm, though it carry with it [Pg 72]the same old facts.

What we want to secure is, not a formidable number of parrot-like statements, but a firm foundation for future clearness of understanding, depth of feeling, and firmness of purpose. So, at the beginning of the exercise, we should not ask John if he remembers what we talked about last time, and expect him to answer clearly at once. Because he does not answer our formal questions which do not properly belong to babyhood, we need not conclude he has learned nothing, for a child can show to our dull eyes only a very tiny glimpse of his wonderful inner world.

Let our aim be, that the child shall little by little receive impressions so clearly that he will recognize them when they appear again, and that he shall, after a time, know these impressions by their names. It is nothing but play after all, but it is in this childish play that deep meaning lies.

A child is far less interested in that which is given him complete than in that which needs something from him to make it perfect. He loves to employ all his energies in conceiving and constructing forms; the less you do for him the better he enjoys it, if he has been trained to independence.[41]

[Pg 73]Pedantry and dogmatism must be eliminated from all the dictations; the life must not be shut out of the lessons in order that we may hear a pin drop, nor should they be allowed to degenerate into a tedious formalism and mechanical puppet-show, in which we pull the strings and the poor little dummies move with one accord.

Yet most emphatically a certain order and harmony must prevail, the forms must follow each other in natural sequence, the blocks must, invariably, be taken carefully from the box, so as to present a whole at the first glance, and at the close of the lesson should always be neatly put together again into the original form and returned to the box as a whole.[42]

[Pg 74]And now one last word of warning about doing too much for the children in these exercises, and even guiding too much, carrying system and method too far in dictation. We must remember that an excess of systematizing crushes instead of developing originality, and that it is all too easy even in the kindergarten to turn children into machines incapable of acting when the guiding hand is removed.

NOTE.

In opening the boxes, it is well to observe some simple form. It is not irksome, but, on the contrary, rather pleasing to the children, who delight in doing things in concert.

BOXES IN CENTRE OF TABLE.

1. Draw the cover out one half space.
2. Fingers of right hand placed on left-hand side of box.
3. Turn entirely over from left to right.
4. Withdraw lid and place on right-hand upper corner of table.
5. Lift box gently and place on top of cover mouth upwards.

[Pg 75]

READINGS FOR THE STUDENT.

Reminiscences of Froebel. *Von Marenholtz-Bülow.* Page 152.
Child and Child Nature. *Von Marenholtz-Bülow.* 145, 146.
Education. *E. Seguin.* 95, 96.
Lessons in Form. *W. W. Speer.* 23.
Pedagogics of the Kindergarten. *Fr. Froebel.* 108-44.
Education of Man. *Fr. Froebel.* Tr. by *Josephine Jarvis.* 40, 41.
Kindergarten at Home. *E. Shirreff.* 12-14.
Kindergarten Culture. *W. N. Hailmann.* 55-66.
Paradise of Childhood. *Edward Wiebe.* 11-16.
Law of Childhood. *W. N. Hailmann.* 35-38.
Kindergarten Guide. *J.* and *B. Ronge.* 5-13.
Kindergarten Guide. *Kraus-Boelte.* 27-47.
Koehler's Kindergarten Practice. Tr. by *Mary Gurney.* 20-23.
Froebel and Education by Self-Activity. H. *Courthope Bowen.* 140-42.
Kindergarten Toys. *Heinrich Hoffmann.* 17-26.
Conscious Motherhood. *E. Marwedel.* 165, 166.
The Kindergarten. *H. Goldammer.* 49-70.

[Pg 76]

FROEBEL'S FOURTH GIFT

"A new gift is demanded—a gift wherein the length, breadth, and thickness of a solid body shall be distinguished from each other by difference of size. Such a gift will open the child's eyes to the three dimensions of space, and will serve also as a means of recognizing and interpreting the manifold forms and structures with which he is constantly brought in contact."

"The inner difference, intimated in the three perpendicular axes of the cube (and the sphere), now becomes externally visible and abiding in each of its building blocks as a difference of size."

FR. FROEBEL.

"The fourth gift incites the child to consider things in their relations to space, and to the forces of nature, and in his play with the bricks he is constantly engaged in efforts to adapt himself to the laws of their nature, while rendering them subservient to his ends."

W. N. HAILMANN.

1. The fourth gift consists of a cube measuring two inches in each of its dimensions. It is divided once vertically in its height, and three times horizontally in its thickness, giving eight parallelopipeds or bricks, each two inches long, one inch wide, and one half inch thick.

2. Like the third gift in form, size, material, and use, it is unlike it in division. In the third gift the parts were like each other, and like the whole, in the fourth they are like each other, but unlike the whole.

[Pg 77]3. The most important characteristics of the gift are:—

a. Approximation to surface in the symmetrical forms.

b. Greater height and greater extension, resulting in a greater possible inclosure of space.

c. The illustration of two philosophical laws, viz., the law of Equilibrium or Balance, and the law of Transmitted Motion or Propagation of Force.

4. Progress is shown in this gift as follows:—

a. In the difficulty of dictation and manipulation arising from the different character of the faces of the bricks, and the many positions which each brick can assume.

b. In the necessity of perfect balance.

c. In a clearer illustration of dimension. In the third gift the parts were equal in height, breadth, and thickness; in the fourth they are unequal, and therefore each dimension is emphasized.

As to progression, the increase of difficulty suits the increase in the child's power of comprehension and receptivity. He is being developed thus far, not by rapid changes in material or greater exercise in number, but by practice with differing forms, each one bringing with it new knowledge and experience. The organs of perception are being constantly made to grow by exercise with intention. We are forming the [Pg 78]scientific eye which can detect differences ever after at a glance.

5. The geometrical forms illustrated in this gift are:—

S { Rectangular
olids. Parallelopipeds.

{ Square Prisms.

P
lanes. { Oblongs.

{ Squares.

6. The fourth gift presents contrasts of dimension and, as to the area of its faces, contrasts of size and their mediation.

What the Child has gained from Third Gift.

The use of the third gift opened to the child quite a new world of experiences, each one of which was pleasant and instructive, combining all the delights of mental and physical activity, imagination, practical industry, and coöperation.

He has gained an idea, distinct in proportion to the skill with which it has been placed before him, of the cube as a solid body having surfaces, corners, and edges; of a whole and its equal fractional parts; of the power of combining those parts into new wholes; and of the fact that form and size are two separate and distinct characteristics of objects. He has also gained new dexterity.[43] His ten little fingers that seemed "all [Pg 79]thumbs" as they arranged so carefully the clumsy little cubes of the Low Wall can now build the Bunker Hill Monument with unerring skill, and can even, with the grave concentration that it demands, drop the last difficult little block cornerwise into the top of the church window.

The child has counted his cubes from one to eight until he knows them like the children of a family, and can divide them into sets of two and four with equal ease.

These are the deeds. As to the new words the little box of blocks has brought him, their number is legion, comprising many terms of direction and position, names of tools and implements, buildings and places.

Truly if the kindergartner has been wise and faithful, the child has gained wonders from this simple unassuming toy, one which is almost too plain and rude to fix the momentary attention of a modern spoiled child, though even he will grow to appreciate its treasures if rightly guided.

Differences between Third and Fourth Gifts.

And now we approach another cubical box, containing the fourth gift, and, on opening it, see that it presents resemblances between and differences when compared with that just left behind.

We notice at once the new method of division, and in separating it find that the parts, evidently [Pg 80]in number the same as before, are entirely novel in form, though the whole was familiar in its aspect. If the child is old enough to understand the process of comparison, he will see that the parts of the two gifts have each six surfaces, eight corners, and twelve edges; but that while edges and corners are alike, the faces differ greatly on the new block, which he will probably call the "brick," as it is a familiar form and name to him. This process of comparison will be greatly facilitated if he models the two cubes in clay, and divides them with string or wire, the one into inch cubes, the other into bricks.

Dr. Seguin's Objections to the Cube as the Primary Figure in the Kindergarten.

Dr. E. Seguin, in his celebrated "Report on Education," says, in regard to the use of the cube as the primary block or figure in the kindergarten: "Had the kindergartners chosen it with their senses, as it must speak to the senses of the child, instead of with their mind, they would certainly never have selected the cube, a form in which similarity is everywhere, difference nowhere, a barren type incapable by itself of instigating the child to active comparison. Had they, on the contrary, from infantile reminiscences, or from more philosophical indications, selected a block of brick-form, the child would soon have discovered and made use of the similarity of the straight lines, and of the difference of the three dimensions. For example: Put a cube on your desk and let a [Pg 81]pupil put one on his; you change the position of yours, he, accordingly, of his. If you renew these moves till both of you are tired, they will not make any perceptible change in the aspect of the object. The movement has been barren of any modification perceptible to the senses and appreciable to the mind. There has been no lesson unless you have, by words speaking to the mind, succeeded in making the child comprehend the idea of a cube derived from its intrinsic properties; a body with six equal sides and eight equal angles."

Answers to these Objections.

With all deference to Dr. Seguin, whose opinions and deductions are generally indisputable, we cannot regard as unwise the choice of the cube as the primary figure in the gifts.

In the first place, Froebel, having a sequence of forms in his mind, undoubtedly wished to introduce, early in that sequence, the one which would best serve him as a foundation for further division and subdivision. This need is, beyond question, better met in the cube than in the brick, which would lend itself awkwardly to regular division.

Secondly, although there is in the cube "similarity everywhere, difference nowhere," and therefore it might be called in truth a "barren type, incapable by itself of instigating the child to comparison and action," we do not introduce it, [Pg 82]by itself, but in contrast with the sphere and cylinder.

Then, when it appears again in the building gifts, "as the simplest and most easily handled form element," the kindergartner has every opportunity to use it so that it may lead the child to comparison and action, and to develop the slowly dawning sense of difference and agreement without which she well knows "knowledge has not yet made the first step." But, if the cube is a form speaking little to the senses of a child, and requiring description by words spoken to the mind, it is evident that we should use great care in dealing with the second gift, lest we run needlessly into abstractions, and strive to give the child ideas of which he can have no comprehension.

Value of the Brick Form.

The "brick" is a form rich in impressions, for we find that every position in which it is placed gives the child a new perception, and the union of these perceptions furnishes him with a complete idea of the object, and of its possible uses in relation to its form.

Dr. Seguin does not rate it too highly when he says: "What a spring of effective movements, of perceptions and of ideas in the exercises with this form, where analogy and difference, incessantly noted by the touch and the view, challenge the mind to comparison and judgment!"

Dimension.

The fourth gift contains all that the three former gifts showed, and introduces differences of [Pg 83]dimension and equilibrium only hinted at before. It also, as Froebel says, "throws into relief the perception of size by showing similarity of size with dissimilarity of dimension and position."

As to dimension, the child built the Shot-tower with the third gift, and knew that it was high, the Platform and that it was broad, the Well and that it was deep, the Wall and saw that it was thick, etc., so that he has a conception of height, length, breadth; but in the fourth gift he is shown these dimensions in a single block. He is thus led from the known to the unknown.[44] They are united and contrasted in one object, and therefore emphasized.

Equilibrium.

As to the law of equilibrium, it is very forcibly brought to the child's attention every time his forms fall to the table when constructed without due regard to its principles.

He soon sees its practical significance, takes care to follow its manifest expression, and to observe with more care the centre of gravity. Great liberties could be taken with the stolid little [Pg 84]cubes and they seldom showed any resentment; they quietly settled down into their places and resisted sturdily all the earthquake shocks which are apt to visit a kindergarten table during the building hour. The bricks on the other hand have to be humored and treated with deference. The moment one is placed upon another, end to end, the struggle begins, and in any of the high Life forms, the utmost delicacy of touch is necessary as well as sure aim and steady hand.

Here comes in, too, a necessity of calculation not before required. The cubes could be placed on any side and always occupy the same space, but the building with the bricks will vary according as they are placed on the broad, the narrow, or the short face. They must also fit together and bear a certain relation to each other.

In the dictations it will be perceived that we now have to specify the position which the brick must take as well as the place which it is to occupy. We designate the three faces of the brick as the broad face, the narrow face, and the short face or end.

Fourth Gift Building.

The symmetrical forms are much more interesting than before and decidedly more artistic when viewed in comparison with the somewhat thick and clumsy designs made with the cubes. The fourth gift forms cover more space, approach nearer the surface, and the bricks slide gracefully from one position to another, [Pg 85]and slip in and out of the different figures with a movement which seems like a swan's, compared with the goose-step of the stubby little cubes.

It is a noteworthy fact that "the buds," as Froebel calls them, of all the fourth gift Beauty forms were contained in those of the third gift, and have here opened into fuller bloom.

The Life forms are much more artistic now, and begin to imitate a little more nearly the objects they are intended to represent. We can make more extensive buildings also since we have an additional height or length of eight inches over that of the third gift, and thus can cover double the amount of surface and inclose a much greater space. In the first play with the gift, the children's eyes, so keen in seeing play possibilities, quickly discover the value of the bricks in furniture-making, and set to work at once on tables and chairs, or bureaus and sofas and bedsteads.

They engage too in a lively contest with the law of equilibrium, and experiment long and patiently until they comprehend its practical workings.

When they understand the fourth gift fairly well, know the different faces and can handle the bricks with some dexterity, the third gift should be added and the two used together. They complement each other admirably, and give variety and strength to the building, whether forms of Life, Beauty, or Knowledge are constructed.

Froebel, however, is most emphatic in directing [Pg 86]that each set of blocks should be given to the child in its own box, opened so as to present a whole at the first glance, and carefully rebuilt and packed away when the play is over. The cubes and bricks should never be left jumbled together at the close of the exercise, nor should they be kept in and returned to a common receptacle.

"Unimportant as these little rules may appear," he says, "they are essential to the clear and definite development of the child, to his orderly apprehension of external objects, and to the logical unfolding of his own concepts and judgments."

"The box of building blocks should be regarded by the child," he concludes, "as a worthy, an appreciated, and a loved comrade."

The mathematical forms are constructed and applied in precisely the same manner as before. The fourth gift, however, offers a far greater number of these than its predecessor, while it is particularly adapted to show that objects identical in form and size may be produced in quite different ways.

Throughout all these guided plays, it should be remembered that time is always to be allowed the child for free invention, that the kindergartner should talk to him about what he has produced so that his thought may be discovered to himself,[45] [Pg 87]and that in all possible ways Group work should be encouraged in order that his own strength and attainments may be multiplied by that of his playfellows and swell the common stock of power. Froebel, the great advocate of the "Together" principle says, "Isolation and exclusion destroy life; union and participation create life."[46]

It is perhaps needless to say that the philosophical laws which govern the outward manifestations of a moving force, as equilibrium or self-propagating activity, are for personal study, and are never to be spoken of abstractly to the child, but merely to be illustrated with simple explanations.

Transmitted Motion.

To show simply the law of transmitted motion, for instance, let the child place his eight bricks on end, in a row, one half inch apart, with their broad faces toward each other. Then ask him to give the one at the right a very gentle push towards the others and see what will happen; the result is probably as great a delight as you could reasonably wish to put within his reach.

When he asks, "What makes them do so?" as every thoughtful child is apt to do, let us ask the class the same question and set them thinking about it. "Which brick did it?" we may say familiarly, and they will see it all in a moment,—where the force originated, how it gave [Pg 88]itself to the next brick in order, that one in turn doing the same, and so on.

This law of transmitted motion, when so simply illustrated in the fourth gift, easily suggests to the children the force of example, and indeed every physical law seems to have its correlate in the moral world. We may make the children see it very clearly through the seven poor, weak little bricks that fell down because they were touched by the first one. They really could not help it; now, how about seven little boys or girls? They can help doing things, can they not?

By such simple exercises and appropriate comments the children may be made to realize their moral free agency.

READINGS FOR THE STUDENT.

Kindergarten at Home. *Emily Shirreff.* Pages 58-61.
Kindergarten Culture. *W. N. Hailmann.* 66.
Koehler's Kindergarten Practice. Tr. by *Mary Gurney.* 23, 24.
Kindergarten Guide. *J. and B. Ronge.* 13-24.
Pedagogics of the Kindergarten. *Fr. Froebel.* 166-95.
Paradise of Childhood. *Edward Wiebe.* 17-19.
Kindergarten Guide. *Kraus-Boelte.* 47-81.
Froebel and Education by Self-Activity. *H. Courthope Bowen.* 141, 142.
Kindergarten Toys. *H. Hoffmann.* 27-30.

[Pg 89]

FROEBEL'S FIFTH GIFT

"The material for making forms increases by degrees, progressing according to law, as Nature prescribes. The simple wild rose existed before the double one was formed by careful culture. Children are too often overwhelmed with quantity and variety of material that makes formation impossible to them."

"The demand of the new gift, therefore, is that the oblique line, hitherto only transiently indicated, shall become an abiding feature of its material."

"In the forms made with the fifth gift there rules a living spirit of unity. Even members and directions which are apparently isolated are discovered to be related by significant connecting members and links, and the whole shows itself in all its parts as one and living,—therefore, also, as a life-rousing, life-nurturing, and life-developing totality."

FR. FROEBEL.

1. The fifth gift is a three-inch cube, which, being divided equally twice in each dimension, produces twenty-seven one-inch cubes. Three of these are divided into halves by one diagonal cut, and three others into quarters by two diagonal cuts crossing each other, making in all thirty-nine pieces, twenty-one of which are whole cubes, the same size as those of the third gift.

2. The fifth gift seems to be an extension of the third, from which it differs in the following points:—

The third gift is a two-inch cube, the fifth a [Pg 90]three-inch cube; the third is divided once in each dimension, the fifth twice. In the third all the parts are like each other and like the whole; in the fourth, they are like each other but unlike the whole; and in the fifth they are not only for the most part unlike each other, but eighteen of them are unlike the whole.

The third gift emphasized vertical and horizontal divisions producing entirely rectangular solids; the fifth, by introduction of the slanting line and triangular prism, extends the element of form. In the third gift, the slanting direction was merely implied in a transitory way by the position of the blocks; in the fifth it is definitely realized by their diagonal division.

In number, the third gift emphasized two and multiples of two; the fifth is related to the fourth in its advance in complexity of form and mathematical relations.

3. The most important characteristics of the gift are: introduction of diagonal line and triangular form; division into thirds, ninths, and twenty-sevenths; illustration of the inclined plane and cube-root. As a result of these combined characteristics, it is specially adapted to the production of symmetrical forms.

It includes not only multiplicity, but, for the first time, diversity of material.

4. The fifth gift realizes a higher unity through a greater variety than has been illustrated previously. [Pg 91]It corresponds with the child's increasing power of analysis; it offers increased complexity to satisfy his growing powers of creation, and less definitely suggestive material in order to keep pace with his developing individuality.

5. The geometrical forms illustrated in this gift are:—

Solids.
{ Cube.
{ Rectangular Parallelopiped.
{ Square Prism.
{ Triangular Prism.
{ Rhomboidal Prism.
{ Trapezoidal Prism.
{ Pentagonal Prism.
{ Hexagonal Prism.
{ Heptagonal Prism.
{ Octagonal Prism.

Planes.
{ Square.
{ Oblong.
{ Right Isosceles Triangle.
{ Rhomboid.
{ Oblong.
{ Trapezium.
{ Trapezoid.
{ Pentagon.
{ Hexagon.
{ Heptagon.
{ Octagon.

6. The fifth gift shows the following contrasts and mediations:—

The diagonal line a connection between the [Pg 92]horizontal and vertical; the right angle as a connection between the obtuse angle (largest) and the acute angle (smallest); in size of parts the half cube standing between the whole and quarter cubes.

We have thus far been proceeding from unity to variety, from the whole to its parts, from the simple to the complex, from easily constructed forms to those more difficult of manipulation and dictation, until we have arrived at the fifth gift.

Effect of the Study of Froebel's Gifts on the Kindergartner.

How instructive and delightful have we found this orderly procedure; this development of great from little things; this thoughtful association of new and practical ideas with all that is familiar to the child mind and heart. Every year the training teacher feels it anew herself, and is sure of the growing interest and sympathy of her pupils.

Many persons who fail to grasp the true meaning of the kindergarten seem to consider the balls and blocks and sticks with which we work most insignificant little objects; but we think, on the other hand, that nothing in the universe is small or insignificant if viewed in its right connection and undertaken with earnestness and enthusiasm. Nothing in childhood is too slight for the notice, too trivial for the sympathy of those on whom the Father of all has bestowed the holy dignity of motherhood or teacherhood; and [Pg 93]to the kindergartner belongs the added dignity of approaching nearer the former than the latter, for hers indeed is a sort of vice-motherhood.

We must always be impressed with the knowledge which we ourselves gain in studying these gifts and preparing the exercises with them. In concentration of thought; careful, distinct, precise, and expressive language; logical arrangement of ideas; new love of order, beauty, symmetry, fitness, and proportion; added ingenuity in adapting material to various uses, æsthetic and practical,—in all these ways every practical student of Froebel must constantly feel a decided advance in ability.

Then, too, the simple rudiments of geometry have been reviewed in a new light; we have dealt with solid bodies and planes, and studied them critically so that we might draw the child's attention to all points of resemblance or difference; we have found some beautifully simple illustrations of familiar philosophical truths, and, best of all, have simplified and crystallized our knowledge of the relations of numbers so that the child's impressions of them may be easily and clearly gained.

Why we are required to study deeply and to know more than we teach.

We have been required to look at each gift in its broadest aspect, and to observe it patiently and minutely in all its possibilities, for the larger the amount of knowledge the kindergartner possesses, the more free from error will be her practice.

[Pg 94]Unless we know more than we expect to teach, we shall find that our lessons will be stiff, formal affairs, lacking variety, elasticity, and freshness, and marred continually by lack of illustration and spontaneity.

Lack of interest in the teacher is as fatal as lack of interest in the child; in fact, the one follows directly upon the heels of the other. For this reason, continued study is vitally necessary that new phases of truth may continually be seen.

Above all other people the teacher should go through life with eyes and ears open. Unless she is constantly accumulating new information her mind will not only become like a stagnant pool, but she will find out that what she possesses is gradually evaporating. There is no state of equilibrium here; she who does not progress retrogresses.

It should be a comparatively simple matter to gain enough knowledge for teaching,—the difficult thing is the art of imparting it. Said Lord Bacon, "The art of well delivering the knowledge we possess to others is among the secrets left to be discovered by future generations."

Relation between Gifts, and their Relation to the Child's Mental and Moral Growth.

These are a few of the technicalities which have been mastered up to this time by a faithful study of the gifts of Froebel; and yet they are only technicalities, and do not include the half of what has been gained in ways more difficult to describe.

[Pg 95]"To clearly comprehend the gifts either individually or collectively we must clearly conceive their relation to and dependence on each other, for it is only in this intimate connection that they gain importance or value."

If the kindergartner does not recognize the relationship which exists between them and their relation to the child's mental and moral growth, she uses them with no power or intelligence. We conceive nothing truly so long as we conceive it by itself; the individual example must be referred to the universal law before we can rightly apprehend its significance, and for a clear insight into anything whatsoever we must view it in relation to the class to which it belongs. We can never really know the part unless we know the whole, neither can we know the whole unless we know the part.

Pleasure of Child at New Gift.

In the fifth gift, which, it may be said, can commonly only be used with profit after the child has neared or attained his fifth year, we find that we have not parted from our good old friend, the cube, that has taught us so many valuable lessons. We always find contained in each gift a reminder of the previous one, together with new elements which may have been implied before, but not realized. So, therefore, we have again the cube, but greatly enlarged, divided, and diversified. When the child sees for the first time even the larger box [Pg 96]containing his new plaything, he feels joyful anticipation, surmising that as he has grown more careful and capable, he has been entrusted with something of considerable importance. If he has been allowed to use the third and fourth gifts together frequently, he will not be embarrassed by the amount of material in the new object.

Lest he be overwhelmed, however, by its variety as much as by its quantity, it might be well before presenting the new material as a whole to allow the child to play with a third gift in which one cube cut in halves and one in quarters have been substituted for two whole cubes. He will joyfully discover the new forms, study them carefully, and find out their distinctive peculiarities and their value in building. When he has used them successfully once or twice, and has learned how to place the triangular prisms to form the cube, then the mass of new material as a whole can have no terrors for him.

How great is his pleasure when he withdraws the cover and finds indeed something full of immense possibilities; he feels, too, a command of his faculties which leads him to regard the new materials, not with doubt or misgiving, but with a conscious power of comprehension.

Its New Features.

At the first glance the most striking characteristics are its greater size and greater number of divisions, into thirds, ninths, [Pg 97]and twenty-sevenths, instead of halves, quarters, and eighths.

These divisions open a new field in number lessons, while the introduction of the slanting line and triangular prism makes a decided advance in form and architectural possibilities.

Importance of Triangular Form.

The triangle, by the way, is a valuable addition in building exercises, for as a fundamental form in architecture it occurs very frequently in the formation of all familiar objects. Indeed, the new form and its various uses in building constitute the most striking and valuable feature of the gift.

We find it an interesting fact that all the grand divisions of the earth's surface have a triangular form, and that the larger islands assume this shape more or less.

The operation of dividing the earth's surface into greater and lesser triangles is used in making a trigonometrical survey and in ascertaining the length of a degree of latitude or longitude. The triangle is also of great use in the various departments of mechanical work, as will be noted hereafter in connection with the seventh gift.

Difficulties of the Fifth Gift.

The difficulties of the fifth gift are only apparent, for the well-trained child of the kindergarten sees more than any other, and he will grasp the small complexities with wonderful ease, smoothing out a path for himself while we are wondering how we shall make it plain to him.

Effect of Good Training.

[Pg 98]But here let us note that we can only succeed in attaining satisfactory results in kindergarten work by beginning intelligently and never discontinuing our patient watchfulness, self-command, and firmness of purpose,—firmness, remember, not stubbornness, for it is a rare gift to be able to yield rightly and at the proper time.

If we help the little one too much in his first simple lessons or dictations; if we supply the word he ought to give; if, to save time and produce a symmetrical effect, we move a block here and there in weariness at some child's apparent stupidity, we shall never fail to reap the natural results. The effect of a rational conscientious and consistent behavior to the child in all our dealings with him is very great, and every little slip from the loving yet firm and straightforward course brings its immediate fruit.

The perfectly developed child welcomes each new difficulty and invites it; the imperfectly trained pupil shrinks in half-terror and helplessness, feeling no hope of becoming master of these strange new impressions.

Arrangement of Pieces.

To return to the specific consideration of the gift, there must be a plan of arranging the various pieces which go to make up the whole cube.

We have now for the first time the slanting line, the mediation of the two opposites, vertical [Pg 99]and horizontal, and by this three of the small cubes are divided into halves and three into quarters. It is advisable, when building the cube, to place nine whole cubes in each of the two lower layers, keeping all the divided cubes in the upper or third layer, halves in the middle row, quarters at the back. Then we may slide the box gently over the cube as in the third and fourth gifts, which enables us to have the blocks separated properly when taken out again, and forms the only expedient way of handling the pieces.[47]

The exercises with this gift are like those which have preceded it.

Exercises of the Gift

1. Informal questions by the kindergartner and answers by the children, on its introduction, that it may be well understood. This should be made entirely conversational,

familiar, and playful, but a logical plan of [Pg 100]development should be kept in mind. A consideration of the various pieces of the gift may occupy a part of each building or number lesson.

2. Dictation, building by suggestion, and cooperative plays in the various forms. With all except advanced children the Life forms are most useful and desirable.[48]

3. Free invention with each lesson.

4. Number and form lessons. In number there will of course be some repetition of what has been done before, but a sufficient amount of new presentation to awaken interest. It is only by constant review and repetition that we can assist children to remember these things and to receive them among their natural experiences, and fortunately the habit of repetition in childhood is a natural one, and therefore seldom irksome.

Errors in Form Teaching.

As to the form lessons, we must remember that our method has nothing to do with scientific geometry, but is based entirely on inspection and practice. It lays the foundation of instruction in drawing, and forms an admirable preparation for different trades, as carpentry, cabinet-making, masonry, lock-smithing, pattern-making, etc. Even in the primary schools, and how much more in the kindergarten, the form or geometrical work should be essentially [Pg 101]practical and given by inspection. Even there all scientific demonstration should be prohibited, and the teacher should be sparing in definitions.

It is enough if the children recognize the forms by their special characteristics and by perceiving their relations, and can reproduce the solids in modeling, and the planes and outlines in tablets, sticks, rings, slats, drawing, and sewing.[49]

LIFE FORMS.

Forms of Life.

We can now be quite methodical and workman-like in our building, and can learn to use all the parts economically and according to principle. We can discuss ground plans, cellars, foundations, basements, roofs, eaves, chimneys, entrances, and windows, and thus can make almost habitable dwellings and miniature models of larger objects.[50]

[Pg 102]The child is a real carpenter now, and innocently happy in his labor. Who can doubt that in these cheerful daily avocations he becomes in love with industry and perseverance, and as character is nothing but crystallized habit, he gets a decided bias in these directions which affects him for many a year afterward.[51]

Objects which he meets in his daily walks are to be constructed, and also objects with which he is not so familiar,[52] so that by pleasant conversation the realm of his knowledge may be extended, and the sphere of his affections and fancies enlarged; for these exercises when properly conducted address equally head, heart, and hand.

Froebel says of all this building, "It is essential to proceed from the cube as a whole. In this way the conception of the whole, of uniting, [Pg 103]stamps itself upon the child's mind, and the evolution of the particular, partial, and manifold from unity is illustrated."

Group Work.

Our opportunities for group work, or united building, are greatly extended, and none of them should be neglected, as it is essential to inculcate thus early the value of coöperation. We have material enough to call into being many different things on the children's tables; the house where they live, the church they see on Sunday, the factory where their fathers or brothers work, the schoolhouse, the City Hall, the public fountain, the stable, and the shops. Thus we may create an entire village with united effort, and systematic, harmonious action. Each object may be brought into intimate relation with the others by telling a story in which every form is introduced. This always increases the interest of the class, and the story itself seems to be more distinctly remembered by the child when brought into connection with what he has himself constructed.

The third gift may be used with the fifth if we wish to increase the number of blocks for coöperative work, and is particularly adapted to the laying of foundations for large buildings in the sand-table. A large fifth gift, constructed on the scale of a foot instead of an inch, is very useful for united building. One child or the kindergartner may be the architect of the monument [Pg 104]or other large form which is to be erected in the centre of the circle. The various children then bring the whole cubes, the halves, and quarters, and lay them in their appropriate places, and the erection when complete is the work of every member of the community.

SYMMETRICAL FORMS.

Forms of Symmetry.

These are in number and variety almost endless, as we have thirty-nine pieces of different characters. Edward Wiebe says: "He who is not a stranger in mathematics knows that the number of combinations and permutations of thirty-nine different bodies cannot be counted by hundreds nor expressed by thousands, but that millions hardly suffice to exhaust all possible combinations."

These forms naturally separate themselves, Froebel says, into two distinct series, i. e., the series of squares and the series of triangles, and move from these to the circle as the conclusion of the whole series of representations. "From these forms approximating to the circle there is an easy transition to the representation of the different kinds of cog-wheels, and hence to a crude preliminary idea of mechanics."

If the movements begin with the exterior part of the figure instead of the interior, we should make all the changes we wish in that direction before touching the centre, and *vice versa.*

[Pg 105]Each definite beginning conditions a certain process of its own, and however much liberty in regard to changes may be allowed, they are always to be introduced within certain limits.[53]

We should leave ample room for the child's own powers of creation, but never disregard Froebel's principle of connection of opposites; this alone will furnish him with the "inward guide" which he needs.[54] It is only by becoming accustomed to a logical mode of action that the child can use this amount of material to good advantage.

Dangers of Dictation.

The dictations should be made with great care and simplicity. The child's mind must never be forced if it shows weariness, nor the more difficult lessons given in too noisy a room, as the nervous strain is very great under such circumstances. We should remember that great concentration is needed for a young child to follow these dictations, and we must be exceedingly [Pg 106]careful in enforcing that strict attention for too long a time. A well-known specialist says that such exercises should not be allowed at first to take up more than a minute or two at a time; then, that their duration should gradually extend to five and ten minutes. The length of time which children closely and voluntarily attend to an exercise is as follows: Children from five to seven years, about fifteen minutes; from seven to ten years, twenty minutes; from twelve to eighteen years, thirty minutes. A magnetic teacher can obtain attention somewhat longer, but it will always be at the expense of the succeeding lesson. "By teachers of high pretensions, lessons are often carried on greatly and grievously in excess of the proper limits; but when the results are examined they show that after a certain time has been exceeded, everything forced upon the brain only tends to drive out or to confuse what has been previously stored in it."

We find, of course, that the mind can sustain more labor for a longer time when all the faculties are employed than when a single faculty is exerted, but the ambitious teacher needs to remind herself every day that no error is more fatal than to overwork the brain of a young child. Other errors may perhaps be corrected, but the effects of this end only with life. To force upon him knowledge which is too advanced for his present comprehension, or to demand from him [Pg 107]greater concentration, and for a longer period than he is physically fitted to give, is to produce arrested development.[55]

MATHEMATICAL FORMS.

Forms of Knowledge.

We must beware of abstractions in these forms of knowledge, and let the child see and build for himself, then lead him to express in numbers what he has seen and built. He will not call it Arithmetic, nor be troubled with any visions of mathematics as an abstract science.[56]

The cube may be divided into thirds, ninths, and twenty-sevenths, and the fact thus practically shown that whether the thirds are in one form or another, in long lines or squares, upright or flat, the contents remain the same. We may also illustrate by building, that like forms may be produced which shall have different contents, or different forms having the same contents.

[Pg 108]Halves and quarters may be discussed and fully illustrated, and addition, subtraction, multiplication, and division may be continued as fully as the comprehension of the child will allow.

During the practice with the forms of knowledge we should frequently illustrate the lawful evolution of one form from another, as in the series moving from the parallelopiped to the hexagonal prism.

It should not be forgotten that whenever the cube is separated and divided, recombination should follow, and that the gift plays should always close with synthetic processes.

Some of the mathematical truths shown in the fifth gift were also seen in the third, but "repeated experiences," as Froebel says, "are of great profit to the child."[57]

We should allow no memorizing in any of these exercises or meaningless and sing-song repetitions of words. We must always talk enough to make the lesson a living one, but not too much, lest the child be deprived of the use of his own thoughts and abilities.

THE FIFTH GIFT B.

There is a supplemental box of blocks called in Germany the fifth gift B, which may be regarded as a combination of the second and fifth gifts, and whose place in the regular line of material is between the fifth and sixth. It was brought out in Berlin more than thirteen years ago, but has not so far been used to any extent in this country.

It is a three-inch wooden cube divided into twelve one-inch cubes, eight additional cubes from each of which one corner is removed and which correspond in size to a quarter of a cylinder, six one-inch cylinders divided in halves, and three one-inch cubes divided diagonally into quarters like those of the fifth gift.

Hermann Goldammer argues its necessity in his book "The Gifts of the Kindergarten" (Berlin, 1882), when he says that the curved line has been kept too much in the background by kindergartners, and that the new blocks will enable children to construct forms derived from the sphere and cylinder, as well as from the cube.

Goldammer's remark in regard to the curved line is undoubtedly true, but it would seem that he himself indicates that the place of the new blocks (or of some gift containing curved lines) should be supplemental to the third, rather than the fifth, as they would there carry out more strictly the logical order of development and amplify the suggestions of the sphere, cube, and cylinder.

It is possible that we need a third gift B and a fourth gift B, as well as some modifications of the one already existing, all of which should include forms dealing with the curve.

Goldammer says further: "In Froebel's building boxes there are two series of development intended to render a child by his own researches and personal activity familiar with the general properties of solid bodies and the special properties of the cube and forms derived from it. These two series hitherto had the sixth gift as their last stage, although Froebel himself wished to see them continued by two new boxes. He never constructed them, however, nor are the indications which he has left us with regard to those intended additions sufficiently clear to be followed by others."

The curved forms of the fifth gift B are, of course, of marked advantage in building, especially in constructing entrances, wells, vestibules, rose-windows, covered bridges, railroad stations, viaducts, steam and horse cars, house-boats, fountains, lighthouses, as well as familiar household furniture, such as pianos, tall clocks, bookshelves, cradles, etc.

Though one may perhaps consider the fifth gift B as not entirely well placed in point of sequence, and needing some modification of its present form, yet no one can fail to enjoy its practical use, or to recognize the validity of the arguments for its introduction.

READINGS FOR THE STUDENT.

Paradise of Childhood. *Edward Wiebe.* Pages 21-27.
Kindergarten Guide. *J. and B. Ronge.* 24-29.
Kindergarten Guide. *Kraus-Boelte.* 81-113.
Koehler's Kindergarten Practice. Tr. by *Mary Gurney.* 25-31.
Froebel and Education by Self-Activity. *H. Courthope Bowen.* 142, 143.
Pedagogics of the Kindergarten. *Fr. Froebel.* 201-236.
Art and the Formation of Taste. *Walter Crane.* 152, 197-242.
Seven Lamps of Architecture. *John Ruskin.*
The Kindergarten. *H. Goldammer.* 85-104, 111-116.
Kindergarten Toys. *H. Hoffmann.* 31-36.

FROEBEL'S SIXTH GIFT

"The artistically cultivated senses of the new generation will again restore pure, holy art."
FRIEDRICH FROEBEL.

"Life brings to each his task, and whatever art you select, algebra, planting, architecture, poems, commerce, politics,—all are attainable, even to the miraculous triumphs, on the same terms, of selecting that for which you are apt; begin at the beginning, proceed in order, step by step."
R. W. EMERSON.

"The sixth gift reveals the value of axial contrasts."
W. N. HAILMANN.

1. The sixth gift is a three-inch cube divided by various cuts into thirty-six pieces, eighteen of which are rectangular parallelopipeds, or bricks, the same size as those of the fourth gift, two inches long, one inch wide, and one half inch thick. Twelve additional pieces are formed by cutting six of these parallelopipeds or units of measure in halves breadthwise, giving blocks with

two square and four oblong faces. The remaining six pieces are formed by cutting three parallelopipeds or units of measure in halves, lengthwise, giving square prisms, columns, or pillars.

2. The sixth is the last of the solid gifts, and is an extension of the fourth, from which it differs in size and number of parts. It deals with multiples of the number two and three also; with [Pg 113]halves rather than with quarters or thirds, the "half" being treated in a new manner, i.e., by dividing the unit of measure both in its length and breadth, giving two solids, different in form but alike in cubical contents.

3. The most important characteristics of the gift are:—

a. Irregularity of division.
b. Introduction of column.
c. Extent of surface covered by symmetrical forms.
d. Greater inclosure of space in symmetrical forms.
e. Introduction of distinct style of architecture.
f. Greater height of Life forms.
g. Severe simplicity of Life forms produced by the rectangular solids.

4. The sixth gift has no great increase of difficulty, and though new forms are presented there is little complexity in dictation. The building needs a somewhat more careful handling, inasmuch as the Life forms rise to considerable height and need the most exact balance.

The child sees solids whose faces are all either squares or oblongs, but of different sizes, viz., oblongs of three sizes, squares of two sizes.

This is the last of the Building Gifts; the child having received sufficient knowledge to be introduced step by step into the domain of the [Pg 114]abstract, the first step being the planes of the seventh gift.

5. The geometrical forms illustrated in this gift are:—

Solids.
{ Rectangular Parallelopipeds.
{ Square Prisms.
{ Cubes.

Planes.
{ Squares.
{ Oblongs.

6. The brick of the sixth gift is identical with that of the fourth, therefore it presents the same contrasts and mediations.

In number the different classes of blocks stand to each other as 6:12:18.

We may add that the brick is the foundation form of the gift, and that we gain the remaining two forms, the square block and pillar, by dividing it in exactly opposite directions.

Introduction of the Gift.

The sixth gift is so evidently an enlarged and diversified fourth gift, that it is well to compare it on its introduction with the fourth, as well as with its immediate predecessor in the series. When the fourth is placed beside it, and the contents of the two boxes brought to view, it is evident at once to the child that a higher round in the ladder of evolution has been reached, and a new and highly specialized form developed. He is fired at once with creative [Pg 115]activity, and his eager hands so quiver with impatience to investigate the possibilities of the new blocks that the wise kindergartner does not detain him long with comparisons, only assuring herself that he notes the relation of the new gift to the former ones, that he compares the two new solids to the brick, or unit of measure, and to each other, and discovers how each has been produced.

Difficulties of the New Gift.

The difficulties of the new gift are very slight, as has been said, consisting neither in dictation, in mass of material, nor in new forms, lines, or angles. Equilibrium alone presents novel problems, but this law the child now understands fairly well in its practical workings, while he has gained so much dexterity in his use of the other blocks that the height and delicate poise of the new forms are added attractions rather than obstacles.

Forms of Life.

The sixth gift far surpasses all the other building blocks in its decided adaptation to the purely architectural forms. The bricks of the fourth gift may be used as a foundation for the construction of large and ambitious structures, and with this additional material, the sixth gift may excel in producing elegant and graceful forms.

The bricks of course admit of a much greater superficial extension and the inclosure of a more extensive space than has heretofore been possible.

[Pg 116]The children will unaided construct familiar objects, such as household furniture and implements, churches, fences, walled inclosures, and towers, with the new blocks, and seize with delight upon the possibilities of the column, which is really the distinctive feature of the gift.

So far, the building of object forms will closely resemble those of the previous gifts, but a step in advance may be made by the children if the kindergartner is complete mistress of the new forms and knows their capabilities. The gift may serve as a primer of architecture if its materials are thoroughly exploited, and may lead later on to a healthy discontent with incorrect outline, with vulgar ornamentation, and with crudity of form.[58]

Froebel himself, who had made exhaustive studies in architecture, and obtained the training necessary to enable him to take it up as a profession, has left us many examples of sixth gift building, which are to be found in all the German "Guides." The structures are no longer rude representations, but have a marked grace and symmetry, and in their simplicity, clearness of outline, and fine proportion, strongly resemble early Greek architecture. Colonnades, commemorative columns, façades of palaces, belvederes, [Pg 117]temples, arches, city gates, monuments, fountains, portals, fonts, observatories,—all can be constructed in miniature with due regard to law, fitness, and proportion, and as the soft, creamy-white structures rise on the various tables, we see borne out Froebel's saying that the order of his Building Gifts was such that the child might be led in their use through the world's great architectural epochs from Egypt to Rome.[59]

Forms of Symmetry.

Although with this gift we cannot produce symmetrical forms in as great diversity as with the fifth, yet the materials are productive to the inventive mind, and when the pieces are arranged with care and taste, beautiful figures may always be developed, those having a triangular centre being novel and especially pleasing. Although not as diversified, however, they have the added advantage of approaching nearer the plane; and that this progression may be more clearly shown, it seems evident that the symmetrical forms should only be produced by laying the columns, "square-faced blocks" and bricks, flat upon the table, and that the practice, [Pg 118]advised by some authorities, of changing the figures by placing the blocks erect, or half erect, should be discouraged.

Forms of Knowledge.

In the forms of knowledge we find again much less diversity than in the fifth gift,—the rectilinear solids and consequent absence of oblique angles limiting us in the construction of geometrical forms. The blocks, however, offer excellent means for general arithmetical instruction, for working out problems as to areas, for further illustration of dimension, and for building many varieties of parallelopipeds, square prisms, and cubes, and studying the parallelograms which bound them. The elements of this knowledge, it is true, were gained with the fourth gift, but we must remember that interest in any subject is not necessarily decreased by repetition, and that the value of review depends upon whether or not it is mechanical.[60]

Coöperative Work.

The group work at the square tables is now especially beautiful, both when forms of symmetry or object forms are constructed. The fourth gift may be used, as has [Pg 119]been said, if more material is needed, and of course combines perfectly with the sixth gift blocks. A large sixth gift made as was suggested for the fifth, on the scale of a foot instead of an inch, is most useful for coöperative exercises in the centre of the ring, and the slender, graceful columns, for instance, which may thus be built in unison to commemorate some historic birthday, are so many concrete evidences to the child's eyes of the value of united effort.

The Gifts and their Treatment by the Kindergartner.

Every gift and occupation and exercise of the kindergarten has been developed with infinite love and forethought to meet the child's wishes and capabilities; every one of them has been so delicately adjusted to meet the demands of the case, and so gently drawn into the natural and legitimate channel of childlike play, that they never fail to meet with an enthusiastic reception from the child, nor to awaken the strongest interest in him.

The kindergartner should be careful that he never builds hastily or lawlessly, and above all she should guide him to those forms which he will be able to construct with perfection and accuracy. She should always follow him in his work, answering his questions and suggesting new ideas, letting him feel in every way that she is in sympathy with him, and that none of his plans or experiments, however small they may be, are indifferent to her. It is always a delight to [Pg 120]the child if his productions are understood by grown-up people, for he often feels somewhat doubtful of the value of his work until the seal of approval has been set upon it by a superior mind.

Underlying Idea of Froebel's Gifts.

If we have grasped the underlying idea which welds the mass of material which forms the kindergarten gifts into a harmoniously connected whole; if we have developed the analytical faculty sufficiently to perceive their relation to the child, the child's relation to them, and the reasons for their selection as mediums of education; if we see clearly why each object is given, what connection it has with the child's development, and what natural laws should govern it in play, then we comprehend Froebel's own idea of their use.

Education *vs.* Cramming.

Certainly the ignorant and unsympathetic kindergartner may err in dealing with them, and introduce the cramming process into her field of labor as easily as the public school teacher, for it is as easy to cram with objects as with books, and should this occur there is cause for grave uneasiness, since the opportunity for injuring the brain of the child is greater during these first years than at any other time.

If we force the child, or make the lesson seem work to him, his faculties will rebel, he will be dull, inattentive, or restless, according to his temperament or physical state; he will not be [Pg 121]interested in what we teach him, and therefore it will make no impression on him.

The child has memory enough; he remembers the picnic in the woods, the glorious sail across the bay, the white foam in the wake of the boat, the very tint of the flowers that he gathered,—in fact, he remembers everything in which he is interested. If we would have him remember our teachings forever, we must make them worthy of being remembered forever. And to this end it is essential that only the best teachers be provided for little children. The ideal teacher should know her subject thoroughly, but should be able to boil it down, to condense it, so that the concentrated extract alone will remain, and this be presented to her pupils.[61]

In leaving these first six gifts, we need finally to remember these things:—

Suggestions as to Method.

First, that we must not be too anxious to resolve these plays into the routine of lessons; with our younger pupils especially this is not admissible, and we must guard against it in all exercises with the kindergarten materials.

Second, we may assure ourselves, in all modesty, that it is a difficult matter, indeed, to direct these plays properly; that is, to have system and method enough to guard the children from all lawlessness, [Pg 122]idleness, and disorder, and yet to keep from falling into a mechanical drill which will never produce the wished-for results. Play is the natural, the appropriate business and occupation of the child left to his own resources, and we must strive to turn our lessons into that channel,—only thus shall we reach the highest measure of true success.

Third, we must strive by constant study and thought, by entering into the innermost chambers of the child-nature, and estimating its cravings and necessities, to penetrate the secret, the soul of the Froebel gifts, then we shall never more be satisfied with their external appearances and superficial uses.

NOTE. In arranging the blocks of the sixth gift, place the eighteen bricks erect, in three rows, with their broad faces together. On top of these place nine of the square-faced blocks, thus forming a second layer. The third layer is formed by placing the remaining three blocks of this class on the back row, and filling in the space in front with the six pillars, placed side by side.

READINGS FOR THE STUDENT.

Paradise of Childhood. *Edward Wiebe.* Pages 27-29.
Kindergarten Guide. *J. and B. Ronge.* 20-31.
Kindergarten Guide. *Kraus-Boelte.* 113-145.
Koehler's Kindergarten Practice. Tr. by *Mary Gurney.* 31, 32.
The Kindergarten. *H. Goldammer.* 105-110.
Stones of Venice. *John Ruskin.*
Architecture, Mysticism, and Myth. *W. K. Lethaby.*
[Pg 123]The Sources of Architectural Types. *Spencer's Essays,* vol. ii. page 375.
The Two Paths. *John Ruskin.* (Chapter on Influence of Imagination in Architecture.)
Discourses on Architecture. *E. E. Viollet-le-Duc.* Tr. by *Henry Van Brunt.* (First and Second Discourses.)

[Pg 124]

FROEBEL'S SEVENTH GIFT

"The properties of number, form, and size, the knowledge of space, the nature of powers, the effects of material, begin to disclose themselves to him. Color, rhythm, tone, and figure come forward at the budding-point and in their individual value. The child begins already to distinguish with precision nature and the world of art, and looks with certainty upon the outer world as separate from himself."

FRIEDRICH FROEBEL.

"Froebel's thin colored planes correspond with the mosaic wood or stone work of early man."

H. POESCHE.

"There is nothing in the whole present system of education more deserving of serious consideration than the sudden and violent transition from the material to the abstract which our children have to go through on quitting the parental house to enter a school. Froebel therefore made it a point to bridge over this transition by a whole series of play-material, and in this series it is the laying-tablets which occupy the first place."

H. GOLDAMMER.

1. The seventh gift consists of variously colored square and triangular tablets made of wood or pasteboard, the sides of the pieces being about one inch in length. Circular and oblong pasteboard tablets have lately been introduced, as well as whole and half circles in polished woods.

2. The first six gifts illustrated solids, while the seventh, moving from the concrete towards the abstract, makes the transition to the surface.

The Building Gifts presented to the child [Pg 125]divided units, from which he constructed new wholes. Through these he became familiar with the idea of a whole and parts, and was prepared for the seventh gift, which offers him not an object to transform, but independent elements to be combined into varied forms. These divided solids also offered the child a certain fixed amount of material for his use; after the introduction of the seventh gift, the amount to be used is optional with the kindergartner.

3. The child up to this time has seen the surface in connection with solids. He now receives the embodied surface separated from the solid, and gradually abstracts the general idea of "surface," learning to regard it not only as a part, but as an individual whole.

This gift also emphasizes color and the various triangular forms, besides imparting the idea of pictorial representation, or the representation of objects by means of plane surfaces.

4. The gift leads the child from the object itself towards the representation of the object, thus sharpening the observation and preparing the way for drawing.

It is also less definitely suggestive than previous gifts, and demands more creative power for its proper use. It appeals to the sense of form, sense of place, sense of color, and sense of number.

5. The geometrical forms illustrated in this gift are:—

[Pg 126]

Squares.

Triangles.
    { Right isosceles.
    { Obtuse isosceles.
    { Equilateral.
    { Right-angled scalene.

In combination.
    { Oblong.
    { Rhombus.
    { Rhomboid.
    { Trapezoid.
    { Trapezium.

{ Pentagon.

{ Hexagon.

{ Heptagon.

{ Octagon.

6. The law of Mediation of Contrasts is shown in the forms of the gift. We have in the triangles, for instance, two lines running in opposite directions, connected by a third, which serves as the mediation. Contrasts and their mediations are also shown in the squares and in the forms made by combination. This gift, representing the plane, is a link between the divided solid and the line.

Step from Solid to Plane.

We have now left the solid and are approaching abstraction when we begin the study of planes. All mental development has ever begun and must begin with the concrete, and progress by successive stages toward the abstract, and it was Froebel's idea that his play-material [Pg 127]might be used to form a series of steps up which the child might climb in his journey toward the abstract.

Beginning with the ball, a perfect type of wholeness and unity, we are led through diversity, as shown in the three solids of the second gift, toward divisibility in the Building Gifts, and approximation to surface in the sixth gift. The next move in advance is the partial abstraction of surface, shown in the tablets of the seventh gift.

The tablets show two dimensions, length and breadth, the thickness being so trifling relatively that it need not be considered, as it does not mar the child's perception and idea of the plane. They are intended to represent surfaces, and should be made as thin as is consistent with durability.

Systematic Relation between the Tablets.

The various tablets as first introduced in Germany and in this country were commonly quite different in size and degrees of angles in the different kindergartens, as they were either cut out hastily by the teachers themselves, or made by manufacturers who knew very little of the subject. The former practice of dividing an oblong from corner to corner to produce the right-angled scalene triangle was much to be condemned, as it entirely set aside the law of systematic relation between the tablets and rendered it impossible to produce the standard angles, which are so valuable a feature of the gift.

[Pg 128]"One of the principal advantages of the kindergarten system is that it lays the foundation for a systematic, scientific education which will help the masses to become expert and artistic workmen in whatever occupation they may be engaged."[62]

In this direction the seventh gift has doubtless immense capabilities, but much of its force and value has been lost, much of the work thrown away which it has accomplished, for want of proper and systematic relation between the tablets. The order in which these are now derived and introduced is as follows:—

The square tablet is, of course, the type of quadrilaterals, and when it is divided from corner to corner a three-sided figure is seen,—the half square or right isosceles triangle; but one which is not the type of three-sided figures. The typical and simplest triangle, the equilateral, is next presented, and if this be divided by a line bisecting one angle, the result will be two triangles of still different shape, the right-angled scalene. If these two are placed with shortest sides together, we have another form, the obtuse-angled triangle, and this gives us all the five forms of the seventh gift.

The square educates the eye to judge correctly of a right angle, and the division of the square gives the angle of 45°, or the mitre. The equilateral[Pg 129]has three angles of 60° each; the divided equilateral or right-angled scalene has one angle of 90°, one of 60°, and one of 30°, while the obtuse isosceles has one angle of 120°, and the remaining two each 30°. These are the standard angles (90°, 45°, 60°, and 30°) used by carpenter, joiner, cabinet-maker, blacksmith,—in fact, in all the trades and many of the professions, and the child's eye should become as familiar with them as with the size of the squares on his table.

Possibilities of the Gift in Mathematical Instruction.

Edward Wiebe says in regard to the relation of the seventh gift to geometry and general mathematical instruction: "Who can doubt that the contemplation of these figures and the occupations with them must tend to facilitate the understanding of geometrical axioms in the future, and who can doubt that all mathematical instruction by means of Froebel's system must needs be facilitated and better results obtained? That such instruction will be rendered fruitful in practical life is a fact which will be obvious to all who simply glance at the sequence of figures even without a thorough explanation, for they contain demonstratively the larger number of those axioms in elementary geometry which relate to the conditions of the plane in regular figures."

As the tablets are used in the kindergarten, they are intended only "to increase the sum of [Pg 130]general experience in regard to the qualities of things," but they may be made the medium of really advanced instruction in mathematics, such as would be suitable for a connecting-class or a primary school. All this training, too, may be given in the concrete, and so lay the foundation for future mathematical work on the rock of practical observation.

The kindergarten child is expected only to know the different kinds of triangles from each other, and to be familiar with their simple names, to recognize the standard angles, and to know practically that all right angles are equally large, obtuse angles greater, and acute less than right angles. All this he will learn by means of play with the tablets, by dictations and inventions, and by constant comparison and use of the various forms.

How and when Tablets should be introduced.

As to the introduction of the tablets, the square is first of all of course given to the child. A small cube of the third gift may be taken and surrounded on all its faces by square tablets, and then each one "peeled off," disclosing, as it were, the hidden solid. We may also mould cubes of clay and have the children slice off one of the square faces, as both processes show conclusively the relation the square plane bears to the cube whose faces are squares. If the first tablets introduced are of pasteboard, as probably will be the case, the new [Pg 131]material should be noted and some idea given of the manufacture of paper.

There is a vast difference in opinion concerning the introduction of this seventh gift, and it is used by the child in the various kindergartens at all times, from the beginning of his ball plays up to his laying aside of the fifth gift. It seems very clear, however, that he should not use the square plane until after he has received some impression of the three dimensions as they are shown in solid bodies, and this Mr. Hailmann tells us he has no proper means of gaining, save through the fourth gift.[63]

As to the triangular tablets, it is evident enough they should not be dealt with until after the child has seen the triangular plane on the solid forms of the fifth gift. Mr. Hailmann says that a clear idea of the extension of solids in three dimensions can only come from a familiarity with the bricks, and again that the abstractions of the tablet should not be obtruded on the child's notice until he has that clear idea.

Though the six tablets which surround the cube may be given to the child at the first exercise, it is better to dictate simple positions of one or two squares first, and let him use the six in dictation and many more in invention.

Order of introducing Triangles.

[Pg 132]The first triangle given is the right isosceles, showing the angle of forty-five degrees, and formed by bisecting the square with a diagonal line. The child should be given a square of paper and scissors and allowed to discover the new form for himself, letting him experiment until the desired triangle is obtained. He should then study the new form, its edges and angles, and then join his two right-angled triangles into a square, a larger triangle, etc. Then let him observe how many positions these triangles may assume by moving one round the other. He will find them acting according to the law of opposites already familiar to him, and if not comprehended,[64] yet furnishing him with an infallible criterion for his inventive work.

The equilateral is then taken up, is compared with the half-square, and then studied by itself, its three equal sides and angles (each sixty degrees) being noted as well as the obtuse angles made by all possible combinations of the equilateral.

Next, as we have said, comes the right-angled scalene triangle, with its inequality of sides and angles, which must be studied and compared with the equilateral; and last of all, the obtuse isosceles triangle, which is dealt with in the same way.

[Pg 133]Here, again, it should be noted that the two last forms should always be discovered by the child in his play with the equilateral, and that he should cut them himself from paper before he is given the regular pasteboard or wooden triangles for study. If presented for the first time in this latter form, they can never mean as much to him as if he had found them out for himself.

Dictations.

The dictations should invariably be given so that opposites and their intermediates may be readily seen. The different triangles may be studied each in the same way, introducing them one at a time in the order named, afterwards allowing as free a combination as will produce symmetrical figures. It is best always to study one of a new kind, then two, then gradually give larger numbers.

Great possibilities undoubtedly lie in this gift, but it is well to remember that with young children it must not be made the vehicle of too abstract instruction. In order to make the dictations simple, the child must be perfectly familiar with the terms of direction, up, down, right, left, centre; with the simple names of the planes (squares, half-squares, equal-sided, blunt and sharp-angled triangles, etc.); and he must learn to know the longest edge of each triangle, that he may be able to place it according to direction.

The children should be encouraged to invent, to give the dictation exercises to one another, and [Pg 134]to copy the simpler forms of the lesson on blackboard or paper. Some duplicate copies in colored papers may be made from their inventions, and the walls of the schoolroom ornamented with them. It will be a pleasure to the little ones themselves, and demonstrate to others how wonderful a gift this is and how charmingly the children use it.

No exercise should be given without previous study, and in the first year's teaching it is wiser to draw or make the figures before giving the dictations. The materials, too, should be prepared beforehand, in such a form that they can be given out readily and quietly by the children at the opening of the exercise. To require a class of a dozen or more pupils to wait while the kindergartner assorts and counts the various colors and shapes of tablets to be used is positively to invite loss of interest on the children's part, and to produce in the teacher a hurry and worry and nervous tension which will infallibly ruin the play.

Life Forms.

The Life forms are no longer absolute representations, but only more or less suggestive images of certain objects, and thus show still more clearly the orderly movement from concrete to abstract.

Hitherto in Life forms the child has produced more or less real objects,—for instance, he built a miniature house, a fountain, a chair, or a sofa. They were not absolutely real, and therefore in [Pg 135]one way merely images; but they were bodily images. He could place a little dish on the table, a tiny cup on the edge of the fountain, a doll could sit in the chair, and therefore they were all real for purposes of play, at least.

With the tablets, however, the child can no longer make a chair, though by a certain arrangement of them he can make an image of it.

The child will notice that many of the forms made with squares are flat pictures of those made with the third gift, and with the addition of the right isosceles triangles he can reproduce the façades of many of the elaborate object forms of the fifth. The various triangles differ greatly in their capabilities of producing Life forms, the equilateral and the obtuse isosceles being especially deficient in this regard and requiring to be combined with the other tablets. The fact that both the right isosceles and right scalene triangles produce Life forms in great variety seems to prove that, as Goldammer says, "the right angle predominates in the products of human activity."

Symmetrical Forms.

The symmetrical forms are more varied and innumerable than those of any other gift, and with the addition of the brilliant colors of the pasteboard, or the soft shades of the wooden tablets, make figures which are undeniably beautiful, and which are mosaic-like in their effect.

The whirling figures are interesting and new, [Pg 136]and the child with developed eye and growing artistic taste will delight in their oddity, and yet be able to find opposites and their intermediates and make them as correctly as in the more methodical figures, where the exact right and left balanced the upper and lower extremes. Here we note that the equilateral and obtuse isosceles triangles, so ill fitted to produce Life forms, lend themselves to forms of symmetry in great variety. The various sequences of the latter in the third and fifth gifts may of course be faithfully reproduced in surface-extension with the tablets, and thus gain an added charm.

The amount of material given to the child is now a matter for the decision of the kindergartner, and is dependent only on the ability of the child to use it to advantage. This increase of material presents a further difficulty, and it is time for us to add still another, that is, to expect more of the child, and to require that he produce not only something original, but something which shall, though simple, be really beautiful.

Inventions in borders are a new and charming feature of this gift, and the circular and oblong tablets as well as the squares and various triangles are well adapted to produce them. The various borders laid horizontally across the tablets may be divided by lines of sticks, and thus make an effect altogether different from anything we have had before.

Mathematical Forms.

[Pg 137]The work with forms of knowledge, as has been fully shown, will be in geometry than in arithmetic, to which indeed the gift is not especially well adapted. In addition to the study and comparison of the various forms, their lines and angles, we have a great variety of figures to be produced by combination. We can make the nine regular forms already mentioned in the introduction in a variety of ways, and thus give new charm to the old truths. We must allow the child to experiment by himself very frequently, and interpret to him his discoveries when he makes them.

The Seventh Gift in Weaving.

The square tablets afford a valuable aid to the occupation of weaving, as all the simple patterns can be formed with them, the child laying them upon his table until he has mastered the numerical principle upon which they are constructed. We can easily see how these same patterns may be further utilized as designs for inlaid tiles, or parquetry floors. Thus the seventh gift may introduce children to subsequent practical life, and serve as a useful preparation for various branches of art-work.

Seventh Gift Parquetry.

It is easy to see when we begin the practical use of the tablets that the essential characteristics of the gifts in their progress from solid to point are now becoming less marked, and that they begin to merge into the occupations, which develop from point to solid. The [Pg 138]meeting-place of the two series is close at hand, and, like drops of water fallen near each other, they tremble with impatience to rush into one.

The inventions which the child makes with tablets he now very commonly expresses a desire to give away, or to take home with him,—a thought which he seldom had with the gifts, wishing rather to show them in their place upon the tables. As this is a natural and legitimate desire, a supplement to the seventh gift has been devised, consisting of paper substitutes for the various forms, of the same size and appropriate coloring, and to be had either plain or gummed on the back. After the inventions have been made, they are easily transferred to paper with parquetry, and so can be bestowed according to the will of the inventor.

Group Work.

The parquetry of the seventh gift lends an added grace to coöperative work, for the children can now combine all their material in one form to decorate the room, or perhaps to send as a gift to an absent playmate. They may make an inlaid floor for the doll's house, a brightly colored windowpane for the sun to stream through, and with larger forms may even design an effective border for the wainscoting of the schoolroom.[65]

[Pg 139]The group work at the square tables is also carried on very fully with the tablets, the symmetrical figures when the colors are well combined being quite dazzling in beauty.

Color with Seventh Gift.

In this connection, a danger may be noted in the treatment of the gifts, both by kindergartner and children. Color appears again here in almost bewildering profusion after its long absence in the series, and is another straw to prove that the wind is blowing strongly toward the occupations. Many of the pasteboard tablets are of different colors on the opposite sides, and though this is of great use in Beauty forms, when properly treated, it is quite often unfortunate in forms of life, unless careful attention is given to arranging the material beforehand. The effect of a barn, for instance, with its front view checkered with violet, red, and yellow squares, may be imagined, or of a pigeon-house with a parti-colored green and blue roof, an orange standard, and red supports. Yet these are no fancy pictures I have painted, and if [Pg 140]the child places the tablets in this fashion, they are often allowed so to remain without criticism from the purblind kindergartner. She even sometimes dictates, herself, extravagant and vulgar combinations of color, such as a violet centre-piece with green corners and an orange border.

There needs no reasoning to prove that such a person is radically unfit to handle the subject of color-teaching, and is sure to corrupt the children under her charge; for in general, if ordinarily well trained, they should now be far beyond the stage in which they would be satisfied with such crudity of combination. They have had their season of "playing with brightness," as Mr. Hailmann calls it, and should now begin to have really good ideas as to harmonious arrangement of hues. If they have not, if they really seem to prefer the pigeon-house or barn above mentioned, then they are viciously ill-taught, or altogether deficient in color sense.

It has been noted that the older children often choose the light and dark wooden tablets, for invention, rather than the gay pasteboard forms; but this may be on account of the high polish of the wood, and its novelty in this guise, rather than because, as has been suggested, they have been surfeited with brightness.

[Pg 141]

READINGS FOR THE STUDENT.

Paradise of Childhood. *Edward Wiebe*. Pages 30-38.
Law of Childhood. *W. N. Hailmann*. 38, 39.
Kindergarten Guide. *Kraus-Boelte*. 145-237.
Koehler's Kindergarten Practice. Tr. by *Mary Gurney*. 6-9.
The Kindergarten. *H. Goldammer*. 116-54.

Kindergarten Culture. *W. N. Hailmann.* 68-70.
Kindergarten and Child-Culture. *Henry Barnard.* 210, 255, 257.
Prang Primary Course in Art Education. Part I. *Mary D. Hicks, Josephine C. Locke.*
Color in the School-Room. *Milton Bradley.*
Elementary Color. *Milton Bradley.*
Color Teaching in Public Schools. *Louis Prang, J. S. Clark, Mary D. Hicks.*
Color, an Elementary Manual for Students. *A. H. Church.*
The Principles of Harmony and Contrasts of Colors. *M. E. Chevreul.*
Students' Text-Book of Color. *O. N. Rood.*
Suggestions with Regard to the Use of Color. *Prang Ed. Co.*

[Pg 142]

FROEBEL'S EIGHTH GIFT
THE STRAIGHT LINE.

The Single and Jointed Slats and Staff or Stick.

"The knowledge of the linear lies at the foundation of the knowledge of each form; the forms are viewed and recognized by the intermediation of the straight-lined."

FRIEDRICH FROEBEL.

"Froebel's laths, wherewith the child can form letters, correspond to the beech-staves (*buchenen Stäbchen*, now contracted to *Buchstaben*, i. e., letters of the alphabet), whereon were carved the runes and magic symbols of our primitive ancestors."

HERMANN POESCHE.

"It will be readily seen how useful stick-laying may become in perspective drawing, in the study of planes and solids, in crystallography; how, while it insures an enjoyable familiarity with geometrical forms and secures ever-increasing manual skill and delicacy of touch, it develops at the same time the artistic sense of the children in a high degree."

W. N. HAILMANN.

1. The wooden staffs of the eighth gift (sometimes called the tenth) are of various lengths, but have for their uniform thickness the tenth of an inch.

They present, as now made, flat sides and square ends, are sometimes uncolored and sometimes dyed in the six primary colors.

2. The previous gifts dealt with solids and [Pg 143]plane surfaces, wholes or divided wholes, while this one illustrates the edge or line.

The previous gifts more definitely suggested their uses by their prominent characteristics; this depends for its value largely upon the ingenuity of the teacher.

We have contrasts of size in the preceding gifts, both in the units themselves and in the component parts of which the divided units are made; but in this gift the dimension *length* is alone emphasized.

3. The most important characteristic of the gift is the representation of the line. The relations of position and form enter as essential elements of usefulness.

4. The laying of sticks may be used as an occupation very early in the kindergarten course, and thus serve as a preparation for the first drawing exercises, but there should be no attempt at this time to give them their legitimate connection with the cube as the edge of the solid and with the tablet as a portion of the surface.

Later they may be introduced in their proper place in the sequence of gifts, and thus assume their true relation in the child's mind. This relation is made more evident as we can and should reproduce the lessons with the solids in outline with the sticks. When the child is more advanced, the connection of the sticks with the preceding objects will be more clearly explained and [Pg 144]intelligently comprehended, and then they may be used in connection with softened peas or tiny corks, which serve to illustrate the points of contact of the sides of surfaces and edges of solids whose skeletons the child can then construct with these materials.

5. The geometrical forms illustrated in this gift are:—

Triangles, quadrilaterals, Angles of every and additional degree. polygons.

Skeletons of solids by means of corks or peas.

6. The law of the mediation of contrasts is shown in the fact that every line is a connection between opposite points. As in the other gifts, the law governs the use of the line in the formation of all outlines of objects and all symmetrical designs.

As we have already noted, the gifts of Froebel are thus far solids, divided solids, planes and divided planes.

Relation of the Single and Jointed Slats to the other Gifts. How both are used.

With the single and jointed slats we shall not deal separately, merely stating that they form a transition between the surface and the line, having more breadth and relation to the surface itself than to the edge, but manifestly tending towards the embodied line of which the little stick given by Froebel is the realization.

[Pg 145]The jointed slats, generally ruled in half and quarter inches for measuring, may be used to show how one form is developed from another,—for instance, the rhombus from the square, the rhomboid from the oblong, and they are very useful also for explaining and illustrating the different kinds of angles, as the opening between the joints may be made narrower or wider at pleasure.

The disconnected slats are used for the occasional play or exercise of interlacing, forming a variety of figures, geometrical and artistic, which hold together when carefully treated.[66]

Materials of Froebel's Gifts.

As to the unpretentious little sticks themselves, the use of these bits of waste wood is entirely unique and characteristic. No one else would have deemed them worthy of a place in school apparatus or among educational appliances; but Froebel had the eye and mind of a true philosopher, ever seeing the great in the small,—ever bringing out of the commonplace material, which lies unused on every hand, all its inherent possibilities and capabilities of usefulness. Froebel was no destructive reformer, but the most conservative of philosophers.

How the Stick is to be regarded.

[Pg 146]The stick of course is to be regarded in its relation to what comes before and after it,—as the embodied edge of the cube, as the tablet was its embodied face. The child should at last identify his stick, the embodiment of the straight line, with the axis of the sphere, the edge of the cube, and the side of the square.[67] The sticks and rings are, properly speaking, one gift, contrasting the curved and straight lines.

Method and Manner of Lessons.

Although the stick exercises should make their appearance at least once every week after their introduction, they may always be varied by stories, and when occasionally connected with other objects, cut from paper to illustrate some point, are among the pleasantest and most fruitful exercises of the kindergarten.

The sticks may be used for teaching number and elementary geometry, both in the kindergarten and school, or for reviewing and fixing knowledge already gained in these directions, for practice in the elements of designing, for giving a correct idea of outlines of familiar objects, and [Pg 147]should constantly serve as an introduction to drawing and sewing lessons, to which they are the natural prelude.

They should be used strictly after the manner of the other gifts, beginning with careful dictations, in which the various positions of one stick should be exhausted before proceeding to a greater number, with coöperative work, and with free invention. These exercises and original designs may be put into permanent form in parquetry, which is furnished for this gift in the various colored papers, as well as for the tablets. The inventions may also be transferred to paper by drawing, and to card-board by sewing.

The exercises may continue from the various simple positions which one stick may assume to really complex dictations requiring from fifteen to twenty-five sticks, and introducing many difficult positions and outlines of new geometrical figures.

Forms of Knowledge and Number Work.

When we consider that the length of the sticks varies from one to six inches, and that the number given to the child is limited only by his capacity for using them successfully, we can see that the outlines of all the rectilinear plane figures can easily be made by their use. Of course in these exercises there must be a great deal of incidental arithmetic, but the gift may also be used for definite number work, and is far better adapted to this purpose than any [Pg 148]other in the series, since it presents a number of separate units which may be grouped or combined to suit any simple arithmetical process. Representing the line as it does, it has less bodily substance than any previous gift, and hence comes nearest to the numerical symbols, as the next step to using a line would obviously be making one. It also offers very much the same materials for calculation as were used by the race in its childhood, and hence fits in with the inherited instincts of the undeveloped human being.[68]

Who has not seen him arranging twigs and branches in his play, counting them over and over or simulating the process, and delighting to divide them into groups? So the cave-dweller used them, doubtless, not in play, but in serious earnest, for some such purpose as keeping tally of the wild beasts he had killed, or the number of his enemies vanquished.

"With a few packets of Froebel's sticks," as has been very well said, "the child is provided with an excellent calculating machine." The use of this machine in the primary school in word making as well as in number work is practically [Pg 149]unlimited; but in the kindergarten it may very well give a clear, practical understanding of the first four rules of arithmetic,—an understanding which will be based on personal activity and experience.[69]

Evolution of the Kindergarten Stick.

It is well by way of prelude to the first few lessons to draw from the children the origin and history of the tiny bit of wood given them for their play, and they will henceforth regard it in a new light and treat it with greater respect and care.

Let us trace it carefully from its baby beginnings in the seed, its germination and growth, the influences which surround and foster it from day to day, its steady increase in size and strength, its downward grasp and its upward reach, the hardening of the tender stem and slender cylindrical trunk into the massive oak or pine, the growth of its tough, strong garment of bark, its winter times of rest and spring times of renewal, until from the tender green twig so frail and pliant it has become too large to clasp with the arms, and high enough to swing its dry leaves into the church tower.

[Pg 150]Then let us follow out its usefulness; for instance, we might first paint a glowing word-picture of the logging-camp, the chopping and hewing and felling, the life of the busy woodcutter in the leafy woods in autumn, or in the dense forests in winter time, when the snow, cold and white and dazzling, covers the ground with its fleecy carpet. Again, let us depict the road and the busy teamsters driving their yokes of strong oxen with their heavy loads of logs to the towns and cities where they are to be sold. A scene, a perfect word-picture, should be painted of everything concerning the trip,—the crunching of the oxen's hoofs on the pressed snow, the creaking of the heavy truck as its runners slip along the smooth surface, the breath of the men and animals rising like steam into the clear, cold air. All these things rise in image before the child's eye and are not soon forgotten, you may be sure. The work and life of the river-drivers might also be described, and their manner of floating the logs down river in springtime when the water is high and the current strong. Then perhaps the children will help to tell us about the mill of which they doubtless know something,—where the sawmills are built, how the water helps in turning the great wheel, the buzzing and hissing of the big saws, and the way in which they quickly make boards of the long, strong logs. This and much more may be said, and if it is well said, no [Pg 151]child can ever look at the tiny stick afterwards and entirely forget the charm which once surrounded it.[70]

Group Work with Sticks.

The sticks are especially serviceable for group work of various kinds, either at the long or square tables. As the children have now an abundance of material they can make all the objects, perhaps, which may be mentioned in a story the kindergartner tells. If it is about the origin of Thanksgiving Day, for instance, Abby, who sits at one end of the line, may make a picture of the Mayflower, and John, her neighbor, make the Speedwell. The next child may construct a cradle for Oceanus, the little Pilgrim baby born on shipboard; the next use his material for the Indian huts the settlers saw after landing; and so on, each child making a different object, which remains upon his table until the close of the story. When this is completed, it will have been fully illustrated by the children with their sticks, and they will be delighted to inspect the different pictures which they will plainly see are much more varied and beautiful than any one [Pg 152]of them could have made alone. Thus the value of coöperation will be plainly shown, without a word from the kindergartner.[71]

Forms of Life.

As to Life forms in general, their number is practically unlimited, though as they are only line-pictures, and heavy lines at that, they are not as real as those made in the Building Gifts. They are easily made, however, and the veriest baby in the kindergarten who handles the sticks as a prelude to his drawing exercises invents with them all sorts of rude forms which he calls by appropriate names.

The question of color as it enters into these forms needs, perhaps, a moment's consideration here. As the gift includes both white and colored sticks, would it not be well to use the former for all dictations in Life forms, reserving the brilliant hues for the forms of symmetry whose charms they would greatly enhance?

Connection of other Objects with Stick Dictations.

We may sometimes connect simple, inexpensive objects with stick dictations, with a view to making them more realistic and delightful. When the little ones are just getting the various positions and corresponding [Pg 153]terms into their minds, and when therefore it is advisable to keep them amused and happy with one to three sticks as long as possible,—that is, until the fundamental principles have become very familiar,—these objects are most invaluable.

Innumerable lessons may be practiced with one stick only, calling it at last a whipstock and giving it a bit of curly paper for a lash. Far from being an instrument of punishment, it makes every child laugh with the glee of possession.

With two sticks laid horizontally we may give a little paper horse-car, or when one is vertical and the other runs horizontally across its end, we may call it a candlestick and snip a half-circle of paper into the semblance of a flame. The effect is electrical, though the light be only one candle-power.

And so on, *ad infinitum*; it is enough to give the hint for the play. We can cut little paper birds for the bird-cages, tumblers for the rude little tables, green leaves for the trees, etc., making the stick exercise, even in its first more difficult details, a time of great satisfaction and gladness.

Complete sets of these card-board objects, one for each child, should always be kept on hand; if well made they will last a year.

Forms of Beauty.

Enough has already been said of the possibilities of the sticks to show that they are most valuable for symmetrical forms. They may be [Pg 154]combined with the tablets, and thus very pretty effects be made, and when four children unite their material at the group work tables, the dictations and inventions produced are of course very large, and may be really beautiful if constructed on artistic principles.

Border work may be very fully carried out with the sticks, and another charming feature of the gift is the way in which it lends itself to the making of snow crystals. These are symmetrical combinations and modifications of familiar geometrical forms around the hexagon. Mr. W. N. Hailmann says regarding them: "At first, it is best to give each child only six or twelve sticks, and to dictate the central figure (a hexagon or hexagonal star) verbally or by means of a drawing on the blackboard. They may then receive a number of additional sticks, and let the central figure grow, all obeying the teacher's dictation, or each following his own inventive genius."[72]

In this gift, as well as in the seventh, the child's imitative and inventive powers are obviously more greatly taxed than in the others, and the danger will be, if he is not well trained, that, as he apparently can do anything with the material, [Pg 155]he will end by doing nothing. The greater the freedom given to the child, the greater the necessity of teaching him to use that liberty in and through the law, and not to abuse it by failing to reach with its aid the highest ends.

Connection of Sticks with Drawing.

We may make the laying of one-inch sticks in vertical and horizontal positions, in angles and squares, a prelude to the drawing of similar lines; and the copying of stick dictations, either from the table, or from memory, into drawing, is a most excellent exercise, calling into requisition great correctness and good judgment, besides an unusual amount of calculation, since the stick dictation will be on a scale of one inch, and the drawing on a scale of one fourth inch, reducing the original design to one in miniature. The child will almost always begin by attempting to make the picture exactly like his model in size without counting the inches and trying to make it mathematically correct; but after the idea is carefully explained and fully illustrated, he will have no further difficulty excepting, perhaps, with the more complicated figures containing slanting lines.

Ambidexterity.

We should encourage in all possible ways the use of both hands in all the exercises with gifts and occupations, not only that one may be as skillful as the other, but also to avoid a one-sided position of the body which frequently leads to curvature of the spine. The well-known [Pg 156]physiologist, Professor Brown-Séquard, insists on the equal use of both hands, in order to induce the necessary equal flow of blood to the brain. Through the effect of our irregular and abnormal development, the cause of which is the too persistent use of the right hand, one lobe of our brains and one side of our bodies are in a neglected and weakened condition, and the evils resulting from this weakness are many and widespread. Dr. Daniel Wilson says: "In the majority of cases the defect, though it cannot be wholly overcome, may be in great part cured by early training, which will strengthen at once both the body and mind."[73]

Abuse of Eighth Gift.

[Pg 157]No materials of the kindergarten (save the beans, lentils, etc., which serve to represent the point) have been so over-used and so abused as the sticks. When no other work was prepared for the children, when helpers were few, and it was desirable to give something which needed no supervision, when inexperienced students were to take charge of classes, when the kindergartner was weary and wanted a quiet moment to rest, when everybody was in a hurry, when the weather was very cold, or oppressively warm, when there was a torrent of rain, or had been a long drought, the sticks were hastily brought forth from the closet and as hastily thrust upon the children. These small sufferers, being thus provided with work-materials in which it was obvious that superior grown people took no interest, immediately lost interest themselves. In riotous kindergartens the sticks were broken, poked into pockets, and thrown on the floor; in the orderly ones they were gazed at apathetically, no one deeming it worth while to stir a hand to arrange them, save under pressure. Sticks had been presented so often and in so tiresome a manner that they produced a kind of mental atrophy in the child,—they were arresting his development instead of forwarding it.

[Pg 158]Such an abuse of material is entirely unnecessary in the kindergarten, where so many ways are provided of presenting the same truths in all sorts of different and charming guises. It is unnecessary and most unfortunate, for it has frequently thrown undeserved contempt on an innocent and attractive gift, which, when properly treated, is one of the most pleasing and useful which Froebel has bequeathed to us.

READINGS FOR THE STUDENT.

Paradise of Childhood. *Edward Wiebe.* Pages 39-45.
Kindergarten Guide. *J. and B. Ronge.* 33-36.
Kindergarten Guide. *Kraus-Boelte.* 239-373.
The Kindergarten Principle. *Mary J. Lyschinska.* 103-20.
Law of Childhood. *W. N. Hailmann.* 39.
Kindergarten Culture. *W. N. Hailmann.* 70-72.
The Kindergarten. *H. Goldammer.* 154-72.
Primary Helps. *W. N. Hailmann.*
Industrial Art in Schools.[74] *Charles G. Leland.*
Drawing and Decorative Design. *Charles G. Leland.*
Art and the Formation of Taste. *Walter Crane.*
Manual of Design. *Richard Redgrave, R. A.*
Principles of Decorative Design. *Christopher Dresser.*
Art and Ornament in Dress. Introduction. *Charles Blanc.*

[Pg 159]

FROEBEL'S NINTH GIFT
THE RING OR CURVED LINE

"Art developed in the same way. The Egyptian temples show us only straight-lined figures, which consequently show mathematical relations. Only in later times appeared the lines of beauty, that is, the arched or circular lines. I carry the child on in the same way."

Friedrich Froebel.

"The curve bears with it in its unity and variety, its rich symbolism to everything which lives and moves, the most intimate relation to that which the child sees, feels, and loves."

Emma Marwedel.

"It might be said that to produce useful objects is the result of the struggle for life; but the tendency to create that which is simply artistic results from no such urgent need, yet it is found wherever the former exists."

Charles G. Leland.

"Thou canst not wave thy staff in air,Or dip thy paddle in the lake,But it carves the bow of beauty there,And the ripples in rhymes the oar forsake."

Emerson.

1. The rings of the ninth gift are made of silvered wire, either soldered or unsoldered, and are whole circles three inches, two inches, and one inch in diameter, with their respective halves and quarters.

2. As the first six gifts emphasized solids and divided solids, the seventh, the plane, and the [Pg 160]eighth, the straight line, so the ninth, the ring, embodies the curve, and illustrates the circumference of the sphere and the edge of the cylinder.

3. All the objects hitherto used have, with the exception of the ball and cylinder, dealt with straight lines and the figures formed by those lines. We now begin a series of exercises with the curve, and the variety of symmetrical figures that can be constructed is immensely increased.

4. Much new knowledge can be conveyed by means of this fresh material, a complete set of new figures may be produced, and the imitation of objects passes from that of things constructed by man, which are mostly rectilinear, to those of nature in which curved lines in every possible variety prevail.

5. The geometrical forms illustrated in this gift are:—

        {
Circles.

        {
Semicircles.

I   {
lanes. Quadrants.

{ Sectors.

{ Segments.

By the union of straight and curved lines (sticks and rings) the entire geometry of the circle may be illustrated, and the child may thus become acquainted with the appearance of the

Diameter.
Radius.
Circumference.
Chord.

Arc.

[Pg 161]6. The law of mediation of contrasts is shown as follows: the semicircles, when placed on the table with ends towards right or left, connect points of opposite direction up and down, and when placed with ends pointing upward or downward they connect the right with the left side.

The circle is of course an unending line traced from a given point back to itself, according to certain laws, but it is also a union of two semicircles curving outward in opposite directions. "It is a representation of the general law, since the periphery and centre stand in contrast to each other, and are connected by the radii."—(Froebel.)

The New Gift and its Charms.

Having already analyzed straight lines in the sticks, we will pass directly to the consideration of the ninth in the series of Froebel's gifts, the rings, which are whole, half, and quarter circles of bright silvered wire.

If the sticks were fascinating to the child as the embodied straight edge or line, and perfect treasure-houses of new possibilities to the kindergartner, the rings are just a bit more delightful as, with their glittering surface and curved lines, and their wonderful property of having neither beginning nor end, they are quite different in appearance from anything which precedes or follows them. Of course the child sees at once that here is an entirely new field for invention, and he [Pg 162]hastens to possess it, fully conscious of his power of combining the new elements.

Introduction of the Ring.

We must first discuss the new form with the children so as to be certain that they fully understand its relation to the other gifts. Perhaps in a previous exercise with the eighth gift we have allowed the children to experiment with a stick, and to break it partially in a number of places so as to produce a measurably correct curved line, afterwards promising them that they should soon have perfect curves to play with. This exercise has its value because it illustrates practically that a curved line is one which changes its direction at every point.

Let us see when to-day's play begins if the children can think of any way to make such curves, save by the stick already used. Some quick-witted little one will remember at once the surface of the ball and his repeated experiments in dividing it, and will suggest in sufficiently plain words that a curved line might be made from a clay sphere. His neighbor thinks a clay cylinder would make one more easily, and both experiments are tried by all the children with a resultant of quite perfect clay rings. Then some one wants to make paper rings, and some one else cloth rings, and the wise kindergartner encourages all this experimenting, knowing that "the power of memory increases in the [Pg 163]same ratio as delight, animation, and joy are connected with free mental activity."

Material of the Rings.

When the wire rings are at last given, some conversation about their material will be pleasant and timely, as it is of a kind we have not had before in the gifts, and shall not have again. The children will see that it is akin to the substance of which their sewing and weaving needles and their scissors are made, and possibly some one may know that both are products of iron. At this juncture it may be well to show a piece of iron, to let the children handle it and note its various properties, and while this is being done, to tell them of the many parts of the world in which it is found, of its great strength and usefulness, and that its value is greater than that of the shining yellow gold. A description of iron mines will easily follow, and the children will delight to hear of the great shafts sunk deep in the earth, of the baskets in which the miners travel up and down, of the darkness underground where they toil all day with pick and shovel, of the safety lamps they carry in their caps, of the mules that drag the loads of iron ore to and fro, and—startling fact, at which round eyes are invariably opened—that some of these mules have their stables down in the ground below, and never come up where the sun shines and the flowers bloom. If there is a foundry in the vicinity of the kindergarten, [Pg 164]and we can take the little ones to see the huge furnaces, the intense fires, the molten iron, and the various roasting, melting, and moulding processes necessary in refining the ore, they will gain an ineffaceable idea of the value of the metal in human labor, and of the endless chain of hands, clasped each in the other, through which the slender wire rings have passed to reach them.

First Exercises.

In the first dictation exercise several whole circles of the same size may be given, and their equality shown by laying one on top of the other. Then we may lay them side by side in actual contact, and the important fact will be discovered by the children that circles can touch each other at one point only. Subsequent exercises take up rings of different sizes, when concentric circles are of course made, showing one thing completely inclosed in another, and next follow the half and quarter rings, which the children must be led, as heretofore, to discover and make for themselves.

With the semicircles, which offer still richer suggestions for invention than the whole rings, another property of the curved line is seen. Two blocks, two tablets, two sticks could not touch each other without forming new angles, nor could they be so placed as to produce a complete figure. Two semicircles, on the other hand, form no new angles when they touch, and they may be joined completely and leave no opening.

[Pg 165]In his work with the sticks the child became well versed in handling a comparatively large amount of material, so that now he can deal successfully from the first exercise with a fair number of whole, half, and quarter rings. We must be careful, however, not to give him too many of these in the beginning, lest he be overwhelmed with the riches at his command.[75]

When the Rings should be introduced.

The rings should not be used freely until the child is familiar with vertical, horizontal, and slanting lines, and not only familiar in the sense of being able to receive and obey dictations intelligently, but in constantly making correct and artistic use of them in his creations. The practice with them, however, is often deferred entirely too long, and the intense pleasure and profit which the child gains from the beautiful and satisfying curved line are not given him until very late in the kindergarten course. This is manifestly unnecessary, for although, if we introduce Froebel's gifts and occupations in orderly sequence, we make greater use of the straight line after the first and second gifts are passed than we do of the curve, yet we should not end with it, nor accept it as a finality; neither should we keep the child tied down altogether to the contemplation of such lines.

[Pg 166]There is no need of exhausting all the possibilities of the straight line before beginning work with the curve, for sufficient difficulties could be devised with the former to last an indefinite length of time.

If the child understands the relation of the edge to the solid, and of the outline to the body; if he is skilled in the use of six to a dozen sticks laid in various positions, he can appreciate perfectly the relation of the curved edge or line to the spherical and circular objects which he has seen in the kindergarten. He remembers the faces of the cylinder, the conversation about spherical and flat rounding objects in his plays with the ball, and he has seen the circular as well as square paper-folding.

He will be accustomed in that to the appearance of the semicircle, segment, quadrant, and sector, and will take great delight in cutting and drawing rings and crescents if we open the way for him.

How we may keep the Curve before the Child's Eye.

Although the gifts, from third to ninth, illustrate straight lines, angles, and rectilinear figures, yet the occupations present many facilities for keeping the curve before the eye of the child. In sewing, we introduce curving outlines during the study of the ball, and work out a series of objects in the vegetable and animal world in order to vary the mathematical precision of the making of lines, [Pg 167]angles, and geometrical figures, as well as to illustrate more fully the spherical form.

We may also use the circular paper-folding in some simple sequence as early as the child's development will permit, and we have, of course, at the very outset, the occupation of modeling, which is one of the most valuable aids in this matter, and the stringing of wooden spheres and beads.

The thread game enters here also, and makes a useful supplement to the rings, as the wet thread may be pushed while it lies on the surface of the table or slate into numberless different forms, all of which may be included under curving outlines.

In linear drawing we give the child lines running in various directions at the earliest possible time, so that he may not grow into a strained and unnatural position of the hand, for this constant drawing of the vertical line, which is necessary to its execution with perfect precision by the young child, limits the freedom of the wrist and muscles, and instead of preparing him to write a good hand, does absolutely the reverse. The various exercises, on the other hand, in drawing the curves of circle and oval and their combinations are quite perfect preparations for clear, graceful penmanship.

We also have, in drawing, Miss Emma Marwedel's circular system, and the outline work performed [Pg 168]by means of pasteboard patterns, most of which are of the curving outlines of leaves, flowers, fruits, and vegetables. When the children can draw quite well from these patterns we always encourage the drawing without them, merely looking at the object to be copied.

These exercises are of the greatest value as connected with modeling when the subjects chosen for invention are comprehended under the sphere, prolate and oblate spheroid, ovoid, cone, etc., the cube with its straight lines coming last of all.

In this way, while keeping up the regular sequence of lessons and occupations with the straight line, we do not debar the child from the contemplation of the line of beauty.

Uniting the Straight and Curved Lines.

After this, he takes great pleasure in uniting the straight and curved lines in his inventions with the sticks and rings given him together, and is quite able to use them separately or unitedly in his creative work. About this time the fruit of these exercises will begin to appear in his drawing. He will attempt to unite his straight lines by curves, and even essay large designs in curves which will be far from perfect, but nevertheless will not be without their value.

Copying Inventions.

The first trials of this kind may be in copying the inventions in rings which he has made on his table, exactly as he previously transferred his stick inventions to the slate. [Pg 169]The spaces should be just as carefully counted, and accuracy expected in preserving the numerical proportions. But this needs much tact and patience on the part of the kindergartner, as well as skill in teaching; for the principles of drawing the curve are much less obvious to the child and much more difficult for him to comprehend than the measurement and calculation of straight lines with their various lengths and inclinations.

These inventions with rings, which are often wonderfully beautiful,—so beautiful, in fact, that the uninstructed person is sometimes skeptical as to their production by the children,—may also be preserved in permanent form by parquetry. It is furnished in various colors for this gift, as for the seventh and eighth, and is greatly enjoyed by the children.

If any should fear that the long contemplation of rectangular solids, planes, and straight lines in Froebel's gifts should tend towards too great rigidity and barrenness of imagination in inventive work, it is obviously within our power, as has been shown, to vary this mathematical exactness, which is no doubt less agreeable to the child than the graceful image of his own fancy (could he attain it), by introducing the curve freely into many of the occupations and exercises with the kindergarten material in general.

Forms of Life, Beauty, and Knowledge.

The rings are of course not as well adapted to the production of objects constructed by man as [Pg 170]were the sticks, but, nevertheless, the material is not without value in this direction. Various fruits, flowers, and leaves may be made, as well as such objects as bowls, goblets, hour-glasses, baskets, and vases. When connected with sticks, the number of Life forms is obviously much increased on account of the union of straight and curved lines thus made possible. Tablets may also be added and contribute a new element to the possibilities for invention.

For symmetrical forms, however, the gift is admirably adapted, since the child can hardly put two rings together without producing something pleasing.[76] Borders enter here in great variety, tablets and sticks being added when desirable, and the group work forms, combining the seventh, eighth, and ninth gifts, give full play to the creative impulses of the child, while calling constantly upon those principles of design which he has learned empirically.

The forms of knowledge which can be made with the ninth gift are necessarily few. It is not especially well fitted for number work, and development of geometrical form is limited to the planes and lines of the circle.

Wooden Rings.

[Pg 171]Miss Emma Marwedel introduced a supplement to the ninth gift in the form of wooden circles and half-circles in many colors. These are much heavier than the metal rings, therefore somewhat easier to handle and give, as she claims, "the child's creative powers a much larger field for æsthetic development." Of course, this larger field is to be found in color blending, not in beauty of design, as the form elements remain the same. The bright hues are undoubtedly a great attraction, however, and perhaps are in line with that return to color which was noted in the seventh gift, when the architectural forms were laid aside. If we adopt the wooden rings we need not on that account lay aside the metal ones, for the two materials may be combined to great advantage.

Difficulties of the Gift.

The gift presents little difficulty, the dictations requiring less concentration than heretofore as the positions in which the rings may be placed are few and simple. Froebel's purpose evidently was that the child should now concentrate his activity entirely upon design, and that he should use the material by itself, and in connection with sticks and tablets to give out in visible form whatever æsthetic impressions he had received through the preceding gifts. The office of the kindergartner is hardly now more than to suggest, merely to watch the child in his creative work, and to advise when [Pg 172]necessary as to the most artistic disposition of the simple material. She may here, if she adopts this attitude, have the experience of seeing the direct result of her teachings, for the child's work will be a mirror in which she can see reflected her successes or her failures.

Froebel's Idea.

The idea of Froebel in devising all these gifts was not, it seems hardly necessary to say, to instruct the child in abstractions, which do not properly belong to childhood, but to lead him early in life to the practical knowledge of things about him; to inculcate the love of industry, helpfulness, independence of thought and action, neatness, accuracy, economy, beauty, harmony, truth, and order.

The gifts and occupations are only means to a great end, and if used in this sense will attain their highest usefulness.

No dictation with any of the kindergarten materials, no study of lines, angles, oblongs, triangles, and pentagons, no work with numbers either concrete or abstract are fit employments for little children, if not connected in every possible way with their home pleasures and the natural objects of their love. Only when thus connected do they produce real interest, only thus can agreement with the child's inner wants be secured.

Actual experiences in the child's life are its most natural and potent teachers. We need constantly to remember that the prime value of the [Pg 173]kindergarten lies in its personal influence upon individuals, and seek to develop each separate member of our class according to his possibilities.

An Objection answered.

The objection has been made that the study and practice with straight lines, angles, geometrical forms, cubes, and other rectangular solids would fit the child for later work in the exact and mathematical sciences more than for other branches of study. But yet it is difficult to see how, when the child's powers of observation are so carefully trained in every way; when he is constantly led to notice objects in nature and reproduce them with clay, pencil, chalk, or needle; when these objects are so frequently presented for his critical inspection and comparison; when he is led to see in the flowers, plants, rocks, and stars, the unity which holds together everything in the universe; when beauty and harmony, mingled freely, constitute the atmosphere of the ideal kindergarten,—it is difficult indeed to see how he can receive anything but benefit from the gift plays, which present at first mainly the straight line, seemingly deferring the curve to a later period when it can be managed more successfully.

READINGS FOR THE STUDENT.

Paradise of Childhood. *Edward Wiebe*. Pages 45, 46.
Kindergarten Guide. *Kraus-Boelte*. 373-417.
The Kindergarten. *H. Goldammer*. 173-78.
The Kindergarten. Principles of Froebel's System. *Emily Shirreff*. 17-20.
[Pg 174]Industrial Art in Schools.[7] *Charles G. Leland*.
Childhood's Poetry and Studies. With Diagrams. *Emma Marwedel*.
The Grammar of Ornament. *Owen Jones*.
Art. *Sir John Lubbock*.
How to Judge a Picture. *Van Dyke*.

[Pg 175]

FROEBEL'S TENTH GIFT
THE POINT

"The awakening mind of the child ... is led from the material body and its regular division to the contemplation of the surface, from this to the contemplation of the line and to the point made visible."

FRIEDRICH FROEBEL.

"And it is precisely thus that the first artistic work of primeval man occurs; he begins by the forming of simple rows, as strings of beads, or of shells, for instance."

"For the last step in this analysis the child receives small lentil seeds or pebbles—concrete points, so to speak—with which he constructs the most wonderful pictures."

H. POESCHE.

W. N. HAILMANN.

1. The point made concrete, which forms the tenth and last of Froebel's gifts, is represented by many natural objects, by beans, lentils, pebbles, shells, leaves, and buds of flowers, by seeds of various kinds, as well as by tiny spheres of clay and bits of wood and cork.

2. We have been moving by gradual analysis from the solid through the divided solid, the plane and the line, and thus have reached in logical sequence the point, into a series of which the line may be resolved.

3. The point which was visible in the preceding gifts, but inseparable from them, now in the [Pg 176]tenth gift has an existence of its own. Although it is an imaginary quantity having neither length, breadth, nor thickness, yet it is here illustrated by tangible objects which the child can handle. By its very lack of individuality, it lends itself to many charming plays and transformations.

4. By the use of the point the child learns practically the composition of the line, that its direction is determined by two points, that the shortest distance between two points is a straight line, and that a curved line is one which changes its direction at every point. The gift closes the series of objects obtained by analysis from the solid, and prepares for the occupations which are developed by synthesis from the point.

5. The outlines of all geometrical plane figures both rectilinear and curvilinear may be illustrated with the point as well as straight and curved lines and angles of every degree.

6. The law of mediation of contrasts is no longer illustrated in the gift itself, but simply governs the use of the material. All lines and outlines of planes made with a series of dots show its workings, and the symmetrical figures, as we have noted from the first, owe to it their very existence.

Meeting-Place of Gifts and Occupations.

[Pg 177]When we begin upon a consideration of the tenth gift, the last link in the chain of objects which Froebel devised to "produce an all-sided development of the child," we see at once that the meeting-place of gift and occupation has been reached. The two series are now in fact so nearly one that the point is much more often used for occupation work than as a gift. This convergence of the series in regard to their practical use was first noted in the tablets, and has grown more and more marked with each succeeding object.

Though the point is in truth the last step which the child takes in the sequence of gifts as he journeys toward the abstract, yet we are met at once in practice by the apparently inconsistent fact that it is one of the first presented in the kindergarten. This can only be explained by the statement that it is in truth quite as much of an occupation as a gift, and is used in the former sense among the child's first work-materials as a preparation for later point-*making* (perforating), and as an exercise in eye-training and accuracy of measurement. It is not an occupation, of course, for the reason that permanent results cannot be produced with it, and because no transformation of its material is possible.

The Point as a Gift.

Before the child completes his kindergarten course, however, he should certainly be led to an intellectual perception of the interrelation [Pg 178]of the gifts and their gradual development from solid to point, for their orderly progression according to law, though it be but dimly apprehended, will be most useful and strengthening to the mind. To discern the logical order of a single series of objects is a step toward the comprehension of world-order in mature life.[78]

The mind in later childhood should be what Froebel describes his own to have been. "I often felt," he says, "as if my mind were a smooth, still pool scarce a handbreadth over, or even a single water-drop, in which surrounding things were clearly mirrored, while the blue vault of the sky was seen as well, reaching far away and above."

When the derivation of plane and of straight and curved line and their place in the gifts are clearly understood by the child, there will be no difficulty in gaining an equally clear apprehension of the point and its position in the series. This may be done somewhat as follows. When the children are playing with blocks on some occasion, we may direct the conversation to the essential characteristics of the cube, its faces, edges, and corners. Do they remember which [Pg 179]one of their playthings is like the face of the cube; do they remember cutting clay tablets from the clay blocks?

It is most unlikely that this experiment will have been forgotten, but if it has been, it may be easily repeated. Speak next of the edges of the cube, and let the children recall the derivation of the stick. That portion of the cube not yet discussed will now be seized upon by the children, and they will ask if any of their playthings are like the cube's corners. Can they think of anything; shall we not try to make something?

Now the clay appears, cubes are quickly fashioned, and each child is allowed to cut off the eight corners of his block. He has no sooner done this than he sees the nearest approach we can make to a point, and proceeds to make a design from them while he recalls the beans, shells, lentils, etc., he has used before in a similar way.

It is well here to suggest making the bits of clay into tiny oblate spheroids, and laying them away to dry so that we may make a group work invention of them to-morrow. Better still, however, is the instant introduction of sticks or wires to connect with the clay points, and thus form at once the skeleton of the solid, which will give an ineffaceable impression of the relation of point and line to each other.

Pleasure of Child in Point-laying and Stringing.

[Pg 180]The pleasure the child finds in point-laying is not confined to the kindergarten, for playing with beads and pin-heads is an ordinary nursery occupation in all countries, and which of us cannot recall long happy hours on the seashore, or by the brookside, when we gathered and sorted shells and smooth glistening pebbles, and laid them in rows and patterns? The mere handling of a great store of these gave a Midas-like delight, and what primitive artistic pleasure we felt as we arranged them according to the principle of repetition to border our garden-beds or to inclose our miniature parks and playgrounds.

The same joy is felt in plucking, arranging, and stringing rose-hips, the seeds of the ailantus, the nasturtium, the pumpkin, or the "cheeses" of the mallow and wild geranium.

Miscellaneous Materials.

It will commonly be found that the child enjoys tenfold more the objects for point-work which he finds himself than the more perfect school-materials. Imagine the joy, for instance, of a bevy of kindergarten children set free on Pescadero Beach (California), and allowed to ramble up and down its shining sands to pick up the wonderful Pescadero pebbles. What colors of dull red and amber, of pink and palest green, what opaline lights, and smooth, glimmering surfaces! "Busy work" with such materials would be worth while indeed,—yet [Pg 181]easy to obtain as they are, they are almost never seen in use.

Smooth, white pebbles, washed entirely clean and sorted according to size, are not uncommonly seen in the kindergartens, however, and are especially useful in the sand-table, and if these and the shining cream-colored shells could be found by the children themselves, their pleasure in them would be immensely increased. That this is true is proved by the experience of many teachers with seed-work. One of our own brood of kindergartners once had a birthday melon party for one of her children. The melons were brought to the kindergarten room and there divided, the small host serving his guests himself. Great interest was immediately shown in the jet-black seeds of the water-melon in contrast with the smaller light-colored seeds of the musk-melon, and unanimous appeals were made to the kindergartner that they might be saved and used for inventions. This was done, and they were always called for afterwards in point-work, rather than the beans, or vegetable and wooden lentils.

In those kindergartens where the seeds of all fruits are saved by the children at lunch hour, it is also noted that the collection thus made is always the object of universal interest and preference.

Use of the Gift.

One of the first uses of the point may be in following the outline of some form of life which [Pg 182]the kindergartner has drawn in white or colored chalk on the child's table. This is much more fascinating work than the placing of seeds one space apart, three in a row, etc., for the latter belongs to the "knowledge-acquiring side of the game," which, as Froebel says, is the "quickly tiring side, only to be given quite casually at first, and as chance may provide suitable openings for it."

The forms drawn in chalk may very well be of curving outlines of vegetables, fruits, leaves, and flowers to connect with the study of the first gift, and may include any other simple appropriate object which the kindergartner is capable of drawing.

The more advanced child can of course make his own Life forms without the aid of drawing, and if he is given different sizes and kinds of shells, seeds, or pebbles, often arranges them with great ability to imitate the shading of the object.

The beginning of the forms of knowledge is in placing the points in regular order on the squared tables at the intersection of vertical and horizontal lines. Next, the child lays one space vertical lines, three points in a line, then two space lines with five points, then horizontal lines, angles, parallelograms, borders, etc., following out the school of linear drawing, and in this way progresses in an orderly manner to the designing of symmetrical forms. Curved lines of course are quite as [Pg 183]easily represented as the straight, and really beautiful designs are often made by the children with them.

Tenth Gift Parquetry.

Tiny circles and squares of colored paper corresponding to the wooden lentils are also to be had with this gift, and afford a means of preserving the designs in permanent form. They are so small, however, as to give occasion for considerable patience in pasting them, and are rather difficult to arrange with regularity without first drawing the design. It is doubtful, in our opinion, if they may be considered to be of any particular educational benefit, if indeed they are not a positive harm to the child in that they require a too minute and long-sustained use of the finer muscles.

Objections to the Gift.

These strictures on the tenth gift parquetry bring us naturally to the criticisms lately made by eminent authorities upon some of the Froebel materials. The objection that many of them require too minute handling and too close attention on the part of children of the kindergarten age seems, as far as the gifts are concerned, to hold especial weight in regard to point-work.[79]

We need not consider here the physio-psychological [Pg 184]tests lately made of the early motor-ability of children and the results which these have shown, but simply concern ourselves with what we have seen and noted many times in daily kindergarten practice. Is it not true that the laying of beans and lentils one inch apart on the tables, for instance, is an occupation which requires very delicate handling on account of the smallness of the object, its easy mobility, and the exactness required to place it precisely at the crossing-point of vertical and horizontal lines? Is it not true that such work requires considerable effort from the kindergartner to make it interesting to the child? Is it not true that there is a cramp of the fingers, shown by a slight trembling, in getting hold of the tiny object and placing it, a cramp of the eye in foreseeing and following the movement, and a cramp of the body accompanying the tension of hand and arm? If all these observations are correct, or measurably so, if they hold with a majority of children, then point-laying as an occupation clearly needs considerable modification in the kindergarten.

What are then the objections to the point as illustrated in bean, coffee-berry, seed, and wooden lentil? In a word, that when represented as above, it becomes too small and too mobile. The difficulty of using these materials is immensely increased by the fact that a slight movement of the child's table will send them all on the floor, [Pg 185]while even an ill-timed cough or sneeze, or puff of wind, will blow them out of position. Point-laying is quite difficult enough for the child's small powers under the best conditions, and need not be made more so by undue mobility in the materials with which it is carried on. This criticism would not hold of course as against large shells or pebbles or as against Miss Marwedel's hemispheres and ellipsoids.

How these Objections may be obviated.

The only good reason for using the small materials to which the preceding objections have been made is a very good one, viz., that if we are to take any concrete object to represent the point, it should be as small as possible, since the point is in reality an intangible something, having no one of the three dimensions. This reasoning seems to be logical enough, and it is surely equally so, to insist that the child shall at some time derive his own points from the cube and make them as small as possible, that he may the better understand their relation to line, plane, and solid. When once this relation is understood, however, and before it is suggested to his mind, why may he not use the larger materials, even though they do not illustrate the point as perfectly? Any lack in perfect representation would probably be more than compensated by the removal of the strain on the accessory muscles and the gain in artistic development. This latter point, indeed, needs special [Pg 186]consideration, for there seems no doubt that the continued use of such small objects for design leads to accuracy and prettiness rather than breadth and power.

The Marwedel Materials.

If we throw out all the smaller materials used for point-laying, and it seems advisable so to do, we still have left smooth pebbles from one half to three fourths of an inch in diameter, and shells of any univalve, such as the "money-cowry" (*cyprœa moneta*). These should be polished, as free from convolutions as possible, and not less than half an inch in diameter. To these we may add Miss Emma Marwedel's wooden ellipsoids and hemispheres, already mentioned, which are satisfactory in size, and add the delights of color.[80]

The hemispheres, which are about one half inch in diameter, come in eight colors and also in the natural wood, are pierced for stringing, and are similar to ordinary button-moulds, having of course one flat side.

The ellipsoids in the six rainbow hues, black gray, brown, and wood colors, resemble elliptical shells, having one flat side, are also pierced for stringing, and vary in length from three fourths of to something over an inch, being nearly an inch wide, perhaps, and a half inch thick.

The children are invariably delighted with [Pg 187]both hemispheres and ellipsoids, and need no stimulus from the kindergartner in their use.

Mind-Pictures.

In some of Miss Marwedel's pamphlets on the use of these materials, she speaks of the mind-pictures which can be made with them, and which are of course quite possible with any of the other gifts. These mind-pictures, showing form and number groups, are drawn by the kindergartner on the blackboard, where they are left a second and then erased. They are then copied from memory, and the results compared, described, and criticised by the children. This constitutes a valuable mental exercise, and if the tests are simple at first and made gradually more difficult will be most valuable in increasing the memory-span as well as in developing language power.

Abuse of the Gift.

If some of the materials used in the kindergarten are unwisely chosen, and if this objection applies in the gifts, especially to the point, then the kindergartner has been, and still is, unnecessarily increasing her sum of error, for no one of the connected series of objects (save the stick) is commonly so forced upon the child. It is somewhat unusual for this reason to find a whole class of children really enjoying point-work, though several conscientious and industrious members of the group may be toiling away with praiseworthy diligence.

Sometimes the children's feeling toward the [Pg 188]gift goes beyond indifference and passes into active dislike, but in either attitude of mind the beans, lentils, etc., are likely to be mistreated.

It is not that the work with them is not in itself pleasing to the child, but that it has been forced upon him *ad nauseam*, and that the kindergartner has lacked interest in presenting it. His own interest has in consequence gradually died out, and when once the fire is cold, who shall light it again?

That there is no need of this abuse of the gift is clear enough, and it can only come from entire lack of originality in using Froebel's materials, or from a mental or physical inertia on the part of the kindergartner, which causes her to prefer giving out such work as needs neither preparation nor previous thought.

READINGS FOR THE STUDENT.

Kindergarten Guide. *Kraus-Boelte*. Pages 439-53.
The Kindergarten. *H. Goldammer.* 181-84.
A System of Child-Culture. *Emma Marwedel.* 6-8.
Hints to Teachers. *Emma Marwedel.* 49.
Decorative Design. *Frank S. Jackson.*
Art in Education. *Thos. Davidson.*
Manual of Design. *Richard Redgrave, R. A.*
Exercices et Travaux pour les Enfants. *Fanny Ch. Delon.*
Manuel Pratique des Jardins d'Enfants. *J. E. Jacobs* and *Mme. von Marenholtz-Bülow.*

[Pg 189]

GENERAL REMARKS ON THE GIFTS

As we close the series of talks upon Froebel's gifts and look back over the ground that has been covered, we see that a number of important subjects have been only lightly touched upon, while we have been altogether silent regarding others equally as vital. This is doubtless inevitable in any work upon the kindergarten which does not aim to be encyclopædic in character, but a few of the more serious omissions may be supplied before we close our consideration of the gifts and enter upon that of the occupations.

First, then, a word on the subject of attention.

Difficulty of holding Child's Attention.

It is not uncommon, when discussing any exercises with kindergarten materials which require dictation or guidance, to hear complaints of the difficulty of holding the children's attention. It may generally be said, doubtless, that when little children fail to give attention it is because they are not interested, and if the teacher finds the majority of her pupils listless, indifferent, and vagrant-minded, she may reasonably conclude that something is amiss either with the subject or with her presentation [Pg 190]of it. The child is as yet too young to command his mental powers and "drive himself on by his own self-determination," and if we enforce an attention which he gives through fear, we lose the motive power of interest which Froebel sought to utilize in the plays of the kindergarten.

Dr. George P. Brown in a late article on "Metaphysics and Pedagogics"[81] says, "Every one admits that there is much that must be done by the child in his elementary education which is a task, for the reason that his ideas of its worth to himself cannot be sufficiently appreciated to arouse a lively and impelling interest in the doing of it," and he adds, "Garfield once complained that he had done so long those things in which he was interested that he was losing his power to do that which did not interest him, which suggests the danger of relying entirely upon interest as an incentive to learn."

That there is a danger here cannot be denied, but it is one which need hardly be considered at the kindergarten age, when that interest which comes from continued agreement between the work in hand and the child's inner wants is absolutely essential to the gaining of knowledge. Mr. W. N. Hailmann puts the whole matter in a nutshell when he says: "If the kindergartner has the penetration to discover these inner wants, and the skill to adapt the circumstances and her [Pg 191]own purposes to these, she will find it easy to secure and hold the child's attention. Without this penetration and skill, all else is unavailing. She may sing and cajole herself into hoarseness, she may smile and gesticulate herself into a mild sort of tarantism, or freeze herself at one end of the table into a statue of Suppressed Reproach,—if the instruction or dictation has no natural connection with the purposes of the children, these will remain uninterested or bored victims of her ill-directed enthusiasm."

Language Teaching.

The plays with the gifts open wide avenues for language teaching if conducted as Froebel intended. He says many wise things on this subject in his "Education of Man," and the following is of absolute application.

"Our children will attain," he says, "to a far more fundamental insight into language, if we, when teaching them, connect the words more with the actual perception of the thing and the object.... Our language would then again become a true language of life, that is, born of life and producing life; while it threatens otherwise, by merely outward consideration, to become more and more dead."[82]

From the first the child should be led to voice his small observations on the gifts in clear language and in approximately complete sentences, [Pg 192]brief though they be. He can as easily say, "I would like a blue ball, please," if asked what color he prefers, as to jerk out a monosyllabic "Blue!"

After a little practice he will use a short sentence when comparing two objects, for instance, but as he naturally moves along the line of least resistance it is hardly to be expected that he will take the trouble to form complete sentences unless gently stimulated to do so. The stimulus must be gentle, however, and given at the right time, for any feeling that his words are criticised will lead him to self-repression, not expression.

In gift work, too, he explains to the kindergartner what he is inventing, and for what purpose; he weaves gossamer threads of fancy about the objects constructed, or describes the forms of beauty and knowledge he has built by dictation.

There is and should be constant interchange of conversation during the gift plays, and the kindergartner who directs them like a drill-sergeant, requiring her recruits only to be silent and obey, has entirely misconceived Froebel's idea.[83]

It is undeniably much easier for the teacher to do all the talking, the children serving as audience, but the ideal to be reached is that she shall [Pg 193]be the audience herself, or rather the chairman of the meeting, guiding the conversation, asking suggestive questions, and making wise comments.

Our language teaching, however, is not confined to the cultivation of greater powers of expression, for there is a direct gain in the child's vocabulary consequent upon his kindergarten experience. He absorbs many new words from his teachers, but many others he learns through his daily work and play, and these are his absolute possession,—the thing and the word together. An interesting series of experiments was once made in the San Francisco free kindergartens relative to the number of new words which the child had mastered and used easily and freely after three years in the child-garden. These included terms of dictation, geometrical terms, names of tools, colors, materials, plants, animals, buildings, and places, new and poetic words of songs, games, and stories, etc., and the experiments established the fact that the child's vocabulary was fully as great as that of his parents and decidedly more choice.

Relation of Word to Object.

It should be said here that there is great value to the child in learning to name things correctly from the very beginning. If the new word is a simple one, he can learn it with perfect ease, and then the object is properly labeled, so to speak, for future use.[84] Familiar [Pg 194]names are sometimes used in the kindergarten when the correct term would be quite as easy to pronounce. This practice often arises from a false conception of symbolism, and is continued with an idea that it is pleasing to the child. Sometimes the pseudonyms are absolutely misleading, as in the frequent speaking of squares as *boxes*, which must, of course, confuse the child as to the real nature of a plane. There are many cases where the geometrical name of a form can easily be taught if it is given *after* the object is clearly understood.[85]

There is a distinction here as to age, which should be noted. Though with babies of three [Pg 195]years it is not only delightful, but necessary, to use objects symbolically, to give play-names to the lines they make, etc., with older children who are nearing the age of school instruction and therefore passing away from the "sense relations of things," it is just as essential to begin a more scientific nomenclature.

Value of Knowledge Gained by Individual Effort.

One of the commonest errors in the kindergarten, as well as one of the most pernicious, is that of assisting the child too much in all his work. This is perhaps more universally true of the plays with the occupations than with the gifts, but even in the latter direction the practice is far too widespread.[86]

The kindergartner often forms his sentences for the child, over-directs him when he is matching colors, gives names to the objects he constructs without waiting for him to do so, moves his blocks, sticks, tablets, rings into more accurate position, changes his spacing when incorrect, rearranges his inventions, selects the colors for [Pg 196]his parquetry work,—and all for what reasons? Primarily, to produce a better effect, it is probable, glorying in the consciousness that the work on every child's table is exactly right, and blind to the truth that uniformity must always be mechanical; and secondarily, to quiet her own feeling of impatience, which sometimes comes from nervous exhaustion and sometimes from an over-eagerness to get a quantity of work done regardless of the method by which it is obtained.

There is a thirdly, too, which is that the inaccurate work, the awkward designs, the unfortunate blending of colors which the little one inevitably makes at first, so offend her artistic eye that she trembles with eagerness to set them right, forgetting that by so doing she is imposing her superior taste upon the child and thereby failing to develop his. We shall never see this matter clearly, nor know how to bear with the crudity of the child's work, until we learn that the crudity is natural and therefore to be respected, and that it is in a sense beautiful after all, for it is a stage of being.

This vice, for it is a vice, of assisting the child too much causes him to lose his own power of bravely and persistently overcoming difficulties, and makes him weak and dependent. It gives occasion for teachers to say, and apparently with justice, that kindergarten children need constant assistance in their school work, that they are [Pg 197]always crying out for help, and seem incapable of taking a step alone.

That this is not true of all kindergarten children we know, but that it should be true of any is a disgrace to our interpretation of Froebel's system, which is, in reality, a very treasure-house of self-reliance, of self-development, and of independence of thought and action.

Value of Interrelation in Kindergarten Work.

One of the highest essentials of gift work is that it should not be isolated from other experiences of the child and concern itself merely with first principles of mathematics, with elements of construction, reproduction, and design, and with unrelated bits of knowledge.

Froebel says in the motto to one of the poems in the "Mutter-Spiel und Kose-Lieder,"—

"Whatever singly with a child you've played,Weave it together till a whole you've made.. . . . ."Thus it will dawn upon his childish soul:The smallest thing belongs to some great whole."

And again,—

"Silently cherish your Baby's dim thought,That Life in itself is as unity wrought."

Nothing is more evident in all his writings, in his more formal works as well as in his autobiography, his volumes of letters and his reminiscences, than that his lifelong struggle was for unity in all things. He would have this unity [Pg 198]expressed in simple concrete form in the kindergarten by a complete interrelation of all the activities of the child; and the gifts as "outward representations of his internal mental world" may be trusted to furnish us with an absolute test as to how far we are carrying out this principle in our teaching.

Whether or not the necessity of correlation decreases as age increases we need not discuss here, but that there is absolute need of it in the kindergarten probably no one will deny. If a single aim does not unify the kindergarten day, (or month, or season), it will be a succession of scrappy experiences, of surface impressions, no one of which can be permanent, because it was slight by itself and received no reinforcement from others. Such instruction only serves to dissipate the mind, to blot out the dim feeling of unity inscribed there by its maker, and to render the child incapable and undesirous of binding his thoughts into a whole.[87]

[Pg 199]What the subjects should be, around which the child's mental, physical, and spiritual activities may crystallize, furnishes a fruitful field for discussion; but, above all, they should be vital ones, for, as Miss Blow says, "Serious injury may be done the mind by developing concentric exercises which belong not to the centre, but the circumference of thought."

It would be fruitless to suggest suitable subjects here, for if they do not, on the one hand, conform to the growing mind of the particular child or class of children, they may either arrest or overtax development, and if, on the other hand, they do not proceed from the kindergartner's insight into principle, it would be but "superstitious imitation" for her to follow them out. No manual, no guide-book, no treatise, no lecture, can supply the want of fine intelligence and judgment in all these matters, and not until the teacher "comprehends the genesis of any principle from deeper principles can she emancipate herself from even the hypnotic suggestion of the principle itself, and convert external authority into inward freedom."[88]

Effect of Froebel's Gifts on the Kindergartner.

Although uninterested and uninitiated persons doubtless regard the various gifts of Froebel as very ordinary objects, made from commonplace materials, yet that this view of the matter is only a peep through a [Pg 200]pin-hole is abundantly proven by their effect on the kindergartner. Those of us who have seen successive groups of young women in training-classes approach the first few gifts have noted that interest is commonly mingled at first with a slight surprise that the objects should be considered worthy of so much study, while underneath lies a half-concealed amusement at the simple forms produced. Yet this attitude of mind endures but for a season, for as soon as the gifts are studied and used practically, it is seen that they contain possibilities of indefinite expansion. When they are looked at through the glasses of imagination, it is wonderful how large they appear, and when one has toiled long hours to invent some sequence with them, one wonders at the reality and fascination of the forms produced.

The outsider who glanced at the materials hastily would undoubtedly suppose them capable of only a limited number of changes and combinations, but the fact remains that every year kindergarten students invent hundreds of new forms with these simple, insignificant blocks and sticks and beans.

How, then, does this change come about? How is it that the same student who once half-scorned the gifts, now, upon the completion of her course of training, looks upon them with affection, admiration, and respect? It is that her eyes have been opened, and whereas she was blind, now she [Pg 201]sees. Her imagination has been awakened, her literary instinct has been stirred, and she has come to look at things in the child way, which is always the poetic way.

Effect of Froebel's Gifts upon the Child.

The effect of Froebel's gifts upon the child has been shown directly and indirectly through the entire series of talks, and need not now be recapitulated. If they are wisely presented and wisely conducted, "inward and outward, the limits of their influence and scope lie in infinity."

Froebel says in one of his letters: "No one would believe, without seeing it, how the child-soul—the child-life—develops when treated as a whole, and in the sense of forming a part of the great connected life of the world, by some skilled kindergartner,—nay, even by one who is only simple-hearted, thoughtful, and attentive; nor how it blooms into delicious harmonies like a beautifully tinted flower. Oh, if I could only shout aloud with ten thousand lung-power the truth that I now tell you in silence. Then would I make the ears of a hundred thousand men ring with it! What keenness of sensation, what a soul, what a mind, what force of will and active energy, what dexterity and skill of muscular movement and of perception, and what calm and patience will not all these things call out in the children."[89]

[Pg 202]It is not that we regard the connected series of gifts as inspired, nor as incapable of improvement, for it may be that as our psychological observations of children grow wiser, more sympathetic, and more subtle, we shall see cause to make radical changes in the objects which are Froebel's legacy to the kindergarten. This we may do, but we can never improve upon the motherly tenderness of spirit with which they were devised by the great pioneer of child-study, nor upon the philosophic insight which based them on the universal instincts of childhood.

FOOTNOTES

[1]"The string unites the ball, symbol of the outer world, with the child, and is the means by which it can act upon his inner nature." (E. G. Seymour.)

[2]"The Egyptians and the Greeks hung geometrical forms over their cradles, so as to strike the eyes of the child with lawful relations. Froebel introduces colored balls for the same purpose, which, considering the psychological and emotional condition of the child, leads to the joyful conception of motion, color, and life." (Emma Marwedel.)

[3]"Suppose, e. g., that the child, by dint of repeated and varied playing with the blue ball of the first gift, has succeeded in getting a tolerably clear notion of the blue ball. If then you bring the yellow ball to his notice, his mind will be led to examine more closely and to compare the two

playthings, resembling each other so fully in every respect, yet differing so widely in color. The other balls of the gift are introduced in judicious succession, offering new yet milder contrasts: these reconcile, combine, the contrasts first offered; they are aided in this by the colors of surrounding objects. The child begins to feel that these color impressions, however widely they differ, have a similar source; he is connecting the contrasts, and as he succeeds in this, he succeeds, too, in separating, abstracting, the *ball* from its *color*." (W. N. Hailmann.)

[4]
"But as he grows he gathers much,And learns the use of 'I' and 'me,'And finds 'I am not that I see,And other than the things I touch.'

"So rounds he to a separate mindFrom whence clear memory may begin,As through the frame that binds him inHis isolation grows defined."

Tennyson's *In Memoriam.*

[5]Many suggestions for the use of the ball in the nursery may be found in Froebel's *Pedagogics of the Kindergarten*, translated by Josephine Jarvis.

[6]See *Kindergarten Chimes* (Kate D. Wiggin), pages 22-32, Oliver Ditson Publishing Co.

[7]"The infant begins to examine forms from the commencement of his existence; for without this knowledge it is doubtful if he could distinguish one object from another, or even be aware of an external world. Gradually he begins to know objects apart and to recognize them, and in time discerns resemblances which cause him to classify them."—W. W. Speer's *Form Lessons.*

[8]Conrad Diehl's *Elements of Ornamentation and Color.*

[9]*Education*, page 130.

[10]"That priority of color to form which, as already pointed out, has a psychological basis, and in virtue of which psychological basis arises this strong preference in the child, should be recognized from the very beginning."—Spencer's *Education.*

[11]"A person born blind, and suddenly enabled to see, would at first have no conception of *in* or *out* (of eye), and would be conscious of colors only, not of objects; when by his sense of touch he became acquainted with objects, and had time to associate mentally the objects he touched with the colors he saw, then, and not till then, would he begin to see objects."—Preyer's*Mind of the Child*, page 58.

"Color cannot be abstracted from that which gives it vitality,—i. e., Form,—from which it cannot be abstracted without rendering the color flat and meaningless." (Geo. L. Schreiber.)

[12]"Finding forms of the same general shape as those taken as types is of the highest importance. Unless this is done, pupils are not learning to pass from the particular to the general. They are not taught to see many things through the one, and the impression they gain is that the particular forms observed are the only forms of this kind. Unless that which the pupil observes aids him in interpreting something else, it is of no value to him. Certain things are taught that through them other things may be seen. Pupils should not be trained to see for the sake of the seeing, but that they may have the power to see." W. W. Speer,*Lessons in Form.*

[13]Emma Marwedel, *Childhood's Poetry and Studies*, page 35.

[14]Professor Earl Barnes, of Stanford University, reports that in his various color experiments on the Pacific Coast, 1000 children having been studied, a very large majority selected red as their favorite color.

[15]"Care should be taken, in the selection of all materials for color lessons, to get as perfect foundation colors as possible; no faded or poor shades are allowable, as they lead the child astray."

[16]"The resemblance of the symbol to the thing signified is a very important matter in education, especially in kindergarten education."—Geo. P. Brown, *Essentials of Educational Psychology.*

[17]"If, therefore, genuine brotherliness, ... consideration and respect for playmates and fellow-men, are again to become prevalent, they can become so only by being connected with the feeling of community abiding in each man (however much or little of it may be found), and by fostering this feeling with the greatest care."—Friedrich Froebel, *Education of Man*, page 74.

[18]"The wooden sphere has no string like the balls of the first gift, because the child no longer needs the outward connection; he now realizes the spiritual connection between himself and the outer world." (E. G. Seymour.)

[19]*Education*, page 132.

[20]E. Shirreff.

[21]"We cannot evolve what has not first been involved."

[22]"Nothing charms us more than the recognition of the old in the new. The man who hurries through a foreign city, indifferent and inattentive to the passing crowd, feels a quick thrill of pleasure when in the midst of all the strangers he recognizes a familiar face." (E. Minhinnick.)

[23]"The infant mind is transparent to resemblance, but opaque to difference."—Susan E. Blow, *Symbolic Education*, page 83.

[24]For second gift songs, see *Kindergarten Chimes* (Kate D. Wiggin), pages 32, 33, Oliver Ditson Publishing Co.

[25]"The sound is a yet higher sign of life to the child, as he then, and also later, likes to lend speech to all dumb things; therefore he also desires to hear sound and speech from everything."—Froebel's *Pedagogics*, page 72.

[26]"But each thing is recognized only when it is connected with the opposite of its kind, and when the union, accord, similitude with this object are found; and the connection with the opposite, and the discovery of the uniting, renders the recognition so much the more complete."—Froebel's *Education of Man*, page 26.

[27]"But now as man both unites the single, which finds its limits in itself, and the manifold, which is constantly developing, and reconciles them within himself as opposites, there results also to the child from both, from *sphere* and *cube* outwardly united, the expression of the animate and active, especially as embodied in the *doll*."—Froebel's *Pedagogics*, page 106.

[28]"On revolving the cylinder on an axis parallel to the circular faces, we find that it incloses a solid, opaque sphere; teaching us the lesson, not only that each member of the second gift contains each and all of the others, but that whatever is in the universe is in every individual part of it; that even the meanest holds the elements of the noblest; that the highest life is even in what in short-sighted conceit we call death."—W. N. Hailmann, *Law of Childhood*, page 35.

[29]"The giving of a new play by no means precludes the further use of the preceding and earlier plays. But, on the contrary, the use of the preceding play for some time longer with the new play, and alternating with it, makes the application of the new play so much the easier and more widely significant."—Froebel's *Pedagogics*, page 145

[30]W. N. Hailmann.

[31]"In each construction the whole of the materials must be used; or at least each separate piece must be arranged so as to stand in some actual relation to the whole. While this awakens the thinking spirit, it also strengthens and elevates the imagination; because amidst so much variety, the underlying unity is made visibly apparent."—Froebel's *Letters*, tr. by Michaelis and Moore, page 72.

[32]"The idea of separation gained here in concrete form becomes typical of that condition which must always exist in any growth—the seed breaks through its coverings, and seems to divide itself into distinct parts, each having its function in the growth of the whole plant." (Alice H. Putnam.)

[33]"If we want to educate children, we must be children with them ourselves." (Martin Luther.)

[34]"What must we furnish to the child after the self-contained ball, after the hard sphere, every part of which is similar, and after the single solid cube? It must be something firm which can be easily pulled apart by the child's strength, and just as easily put together again. Therefore it must also be something which is simple, yet multiform; and what should this be, after what we have perceived up to this point, and in view of what the surrounding world affords us, but the cube divided through the centre by three planes perpendicular to one another."—Froebel's *Pedagogics*.

[35]"*Unmaking* is as important as *making* to the child. His destructive energy is as essential to him as his power of construction." (W. T. Harris.)

"The child wishes to discover the inside of the thing, being urged to this by an impulse he has not given to himself,—the impulse which, rightly recognized and rightly guided, seeks to know God in all his works.... Where can the child seek for satisfaction of his impulse to research but from the thing itself?"—Friedrich Froebel, *Education of Man*.

[36]"An element which slumbers like a viper under roses is that which is now so frequently provided as a plaything for children; it is, in a word, the already too complex and ornate, too finished toy. The child can begin no new thing with it, cannot produce enough variety by means of it; his power of creative imagination, his power of giving outward form to his own idea, are thus actually deadened."—Froebel's *Pedagogics*.

[37]"One of the greatest and most universal delights of children is to construct for themselves a habitation of some sort, either in the garden or indoors, where chairs have generally to serve their purpose. Instinct leads them, as it does all animals, to procure shelter and protection for their persons, individual outward self-existence and independence."—Bertha von Marenholtz-Bülow, *Child and Child Nature*.

[38]"The building or piling up is with the child, as with the development of the human race, and as with the fixed forms in Nature, the first."—Froebel's *Education of Man*.

"Towers, pyramids, up, up, connecting themselves with something high, voicing aspiration."

[39]"The representation of facts and circumstances of history, of geography, and especially of every-day life, by means of building, I hold to be in the highest degree important for children, even if these representations are imperfect and fall far short of their originals. The eye is at all events aroused and stimulated to observe with greater precision than before the object that has been represented.... And thus, by means of perhaps a quite imperfect outward representation, the inner perception is made more perfect."—Froebel's *Letters*, tr. by Michaelis and Moore, page 99.

[40]See *Kindergarten Chimes* (Kate D. Wiggin), Oliver Ditson Publishing Co.: "Building Song," pages 34, 35; "Trade Game," page 70; "The Carpenter," page 92.

[41]"Probably the chief wish of children is to do things for themselves, instead of to have things done for them. They would gladly live in a Paradise of the Home-made. For example, when we read how the 'prentices of London used to skate on sharp bones of animals, which they bound about their feet, we also wished, at least, to try that plan, rather than to wear skates bought in shops." (Andrew Lang.)

"Complete toys hinder the activity of children, encourage laziness and thoughtlessness, and do them more harm than can be told. The active tendency in them turns to the distortion of what is complete, and so becomes destructive."

"Any fusing together of lessons, work, and play, is possible only when the objects with which the child plays allow room for independent mental and bodily activity, i. e., when they are not themselves complete in the child's hand. Had man found everything in the world fixed and prepared for use; had all means of culture, of satisfaction for the spiritual and material wants of his nature, been ready to his hand, there would have been no development, no civilization of the human race."

[42]"In order to furnish to the child at once clearly and definitely the *impression of the whole*, of *the self-contained*, the plaything before it is given to the child for his own free use must be opened as follows.... It will thus appear before the observing child as a cube closely united, yet easily separated and again restored."—Froebel's *Pedagogics*, pages 123, 124.

[43]"A child trained for one year in a kindergarten would acquire a skillful use of his hands and a habit of accurate measurement of the eye which would be his possession through life." (W. T. Harris.)

[44]"The three principal dimensions of space, which in the cube only make themselves known as differences of position, in the fourth gift become more prominent and manifest themselves as differences of size. These three relations of size are in the fourth gift as abiding and changeless as the position of the three principal directions was before and still is."—Froebel's *Pedagogics*, page 189.

[45]"The child is allowed the greatest possible freedom of invention; the experience of the adult only accompanies and explains."—Froebel's *Pedagogics*, page 130.

[46]*Pedagogics*, page 180.

[47]"This procedure is by no means intended merely to make the withdrawal of the box easy for the child, but, on the contrary, brings to him much inner profit. It is well for him to receive his playthings in an orderly manner—not to have them tossed to him as fodder is tossed to animals. It is good for the child to begin his play with the perception of a whole, a simple self-contained unit, and from this unity to develop his representations. Finally, it is essential that the playing child should receive his material so arranged that its various elements are discernible, and that by seeing them his mind may unconsciously form plans for using them. Receiving his material thus arranged, the child will use it with ever-recurrent and increasing satisfaction, and his play will produce far more abiding results than the play of one whose material lies before him like a heap of cobblestones."—Froebel's *Pedagogics*, page 205.

[48]"The child, in a word, follows the same path as the man, and advances from use to beauty and from beauty to truth."—Froebel's *Pedagogics*, page 219.

[49]"The Conference recommends that the child's geometrical education should begin as early as possible; in the kindergarten, if he attends a kindergarten, or if not, in the primary school. He should at first gain familiarity through the senses with simple geometrical figures and forms, plane and solid; should handle, draw, measure, and model them; and should gradually learn some of their simpler properties and relations."—*Report of Committee of Ten*, page 110.

[50]"The child's life moves from the house and its living-rooms, through kitchen and cellar, through yard and garden, to the wider space and activity of street and market, and this expansion of life is clearly reflected in the order and development of his productions."—Froebel's *Pedagogics*, page 221.

[51]"In some German kindergartens large building-logs are supplied in one corner of the play garden. These logs are a foot or more in length, three inches wide, and one inch thick.

Several hundred of these are kept neatly piled against the fence, and the children are expected to leave them in good order. This bit of voluntary discipline has its good uses on the playground, and the free building allowed with this larger material gives rise to individual effort, and tests the power of the children in a way which makes the later, more organized work at the tables far more full of meaning."—*Kindergarten Magazine*, November, 1894.

[52]"As these building gifts afford a means of clearing the perceptions of the child, they give occasion for extending these perceptions, and for representing in their essential parts objects of which the child has only heard."—Froebel's *Pedagogics*, page 222.

[53]"With these forms of beauty it is above all important that they be developed one from another. Each form in the series should be a modification or transformation of its predecessor. No form should be entirely destroyed. It is also essential that the series should be developed so that each step should show either an evolution into greater manifoldness and variety, or a return to greater simplicity."—Froebel's *Pedagogics*, page 225.

[54]"This free activity ... is only possible when the law of free creativeness is known and applied; for that a free creativeness only can be a lawful one, we are taught by the smallest blade of grass, whose development takes place only according to immutable laws."—*Reminiscences of Froebel*, page 133.

[55]"Whoever sacrifices health to wisdom has generally sacrificed wisdom, too." (Jean Paul.)

[56]"Perceptions and recognitions which are with difficulty gained from *words* are easily gained from facts and deeds. Through actual experience the child gains in a trice a total concept, whereas the same concept expressed in words would be only grasped in a partial manner. The rare merit, the vivifying influence of this play-material is that, through the representations it makes possible, concepts are recognized at once in their wholeness and unity, whereas such an idea of a whole can only very gradually be gained from its verbal expression. It must, however, be added that later, through words, the concept can be brought into higher and clearer consciousness."—Froebel's *Pedagogics*, page 206.

[57]"It is through frequent return to a subject and intense activity upon it for short periods, that it 'soaks in' and becomes influential in the building of character. Especially is this true if the principles of apperception and concentration are not forgotten by the teacher in working upon the disciplinary subjects." (Geo. P. Brown.)

[58]"The sense of beauty must be awakened in the soul in childhood if in later life he is to create the beautiful."—*Reminiscences of Froebel*, page 158.

[59]"As the gifts proceed from the first to the sixth, observation is demanded with increasing strictness, relativity more and more appreciated, and the opportunity afforded for endless manifestations of the constructive faculty, while all the time impressions are forming in the mind which in due time will bear rich fruits of mathematical and practical knowledge as well as æsthetic culture, for the dawning sense of the beautiful as well as of the true is gaining consistency and power." (Karl Froebel.)

[60]"What makes Froebel's gifts particularly instructive is, indeed, the fact that the most varied materials constantly lead to the same observations, but always under different conditions, so that we obtain the necessary repetitions without the dryness, the tiresomeness, the fatigue inseparable from constant unvaried iteration. But they also accustom the child to discover similarity in things that appear to differ, to find resemblance in contrasts, unity in diversity, connection in what appears unconnected."—H. Goldammer's *The Kindergarten*, page 109.

[61]"If you would be pungent, be brief; for it is with words as with sunbeams,—the more they are condensed the deeper they burn."

[62]*Pamphlet on the Seventh Gift.* (Milton Bradley Co.)

[63]"The perception of the difference between a surface-extension and an extension in three dimensions begins late and is established slowly."—W. Preyer, *The Mind of the Child*, page 180.

[64]"With this law I give children a guide for creating, and because it is the law according to which they, as creatures of God, have themselves been created, they can easily apply it. It is born with them."—*Reminiscences of Froebel*, page 73.

[65]"The utility of this united action is not to be overlooked. The children all proceed according to one and the same law, they all work to produce one and the same result, the same purpose unites them all; in short, we see here in the children's play all that forms the base of every human society, all that renders it possible for men to act together in organized communities, such as are the family, the state, and the church. And to prepare for the future, to be mindful even amidst play of that which a child will afterwards require in order worthily to fill his place in the world, ought surely not to be among the least important ends of an education

claiming to be in conformity with nature and reason."—H. Goldammer, *The Kindergarten*, page 135.

[66]"The slats form, in some sort, the transition from the surface-pictures of the laying-tablets to the lineal representations of the laying-sticks, but have this advantage over both tablets and sticks, that the forms constructed with them are not bound down to the surface of the table, but possess sufficient solidity to bear being removed from it."—H. Goldammer, *The Kindergarten*, page 155.

[67]"Just as we obtained the tablets from the cubes, of which they are the embodied faces, so now we obtain also the laying-sticks from the cube, whose edges they represent. But they are contained also in the laying-tablets, for one may regard the surface as produced by the progressive movement of a line, and this may be made clear to the child by slicing a square tablet into a number of sticks."—H. Goldammer, *The Kindergarten*, page 161.

[68]"Each following generation and each following individual man is to pass through the whole earlier development and cultivation of the human race,—and he does pass it; otherwise he would not understand the world past and present,—but not by the dead way of imitation, of copying, but by the living way of individual, free, active development and cultivation."—Friedrich Froebel, *Education of Man*, page 11.

[69]"Thus the child's sphere of knowledge, the world of his life, is again extended by the observation and recognition, by the development and cultivation, of the capacity of number; and an essential need of his inner nature, a certain yearning of his spirit, are thereby satisfied.... The knowledge of the relations of quantity extraordinarily heightens the life of the child."—Friedrich Froebel, *Education of Man*, page 45.

[70]"These terse graphic descriptions of objects will be found very serviceable in sharpening and intensifying the powers of observation, as well as securing clearness, distinctness, accuracy, and life in verbal description. Here the pupil learns practically to give due prominence to essentials, and to appreciate the full value of accessories; to look for and discover the fundamental ideas of which things are the modified, adorned, garbled, or stunted expression; to seek and find the very soul of things."—W. N. Hailmann, *Primary Helps*, page 17.

[71]"In this group work it is desirable that the common aims should be fully within the comprehension of each little worker, yet sufficiently beyond his powers of execution and endurance to make him sensible of the need of assistance. The former secures the possibility of individual enjoyment, and hence the only reliable incentive to persistence; the latter insures free subordination to the will of the whole, the essential condition of success."—W. N. Hailmann, *Primary Helps*, page 18.

[72]"These forms are invaluable even as *silent* teachers of geometrical and numerical relations. Used judiciously in conversational lessons, leading to partial or complete analysis of the figures in spoken or written descriptions, their teaching power is inexhaustible."—W. N. Hailmann's *Primary Helps*, page 21.

[73]"Whenever the early and persistent cultivation of the full use of both hands has been accomplished, the result is greater efficiency, without any corresponding awkwardness or defect. In certain arts and professions, both hands are necessarily called into play. The skillful surgeon finds an enormous advantage in being able to transfer his instrument from one hand to the other. The dentist has to multiply instruments to make up for the lack of such acquired power. The fencer who can transfer his weapon to the left hand places his adversary at a disadvantage. The lumberer finds it indispensable, in the operation of his woodcraft, to learn to chop timber right-and-left-handed; and the carpenter may be frequently seen using the saw and hammer in either hand, and thereby not only resting his arm, but greatly facilitating his work. In all the fine arts the mastery of both hands is advantageous. The sculptor, the carver, the draughtsman, the engraver, the cameo-cutter, each has recourse at times to the left hand for special manipulative dexterity; the pianist depends little less on the left hand than on the right; and as for the organist, with the numerous pedals and stops of the modern grand organ, a quadrumanous musician would still find reason to envy the ampler scope which a Briareus could command."—Dr. Daniel Wilson, *Left-Handedness. A Hint for Educators.*

[74]Circulars of Information of the Bureau of Education, No. 4, 1882.

[75]"The number of rings should only gradually be augmented. Satiety destroys every impulse of creation."—Emma Marwedel,*Childhood's Poetry and Studies*, page 15.

[76]"It is true that the child produces forms of beauty with other material also, but it is the curved line which offers the strongest inducements to attempt such forms, since even the simplest combinations of a small number of semicircles and circles yield figures bearing the stamp of beauty."—H. Goldammer's *The Kindergarten*, page 177.

[77]Circulars of Information of the Bureau of Education, No. 4, 1882.

60

[78]"This coming-out of the child from the outer and superficial and his entrance into the inner view of things, which, because it is inner, leads to recognition, insight, and consciousness,—this coming-out of the child from the house-order to the higher world-order makes the boy a scholar."—Friedrich Froebel,*Education of Man*, page 79.

[79]The development of motor-ability in children and its furtherance or arrest by the kindergarten materials concerns the occupations more particularly, and as such will receive full consideration in a later volume.

[80]*Marwedel's Materials for Child-Culture*. D. C. Heath & Co.

[81]*Public School Journal*, July, 1895.

[82]*Education of Man*, page 145.

[83]It is a difficult thing to find the *via media* between complete silence on the part of the children save when answering questions and a confusion of tongues like that at the building of Babel, but there is such a *via media*, and it can be found by those who seek it diligently.

[84]"At all stages of learning the mother tongue, the purely verbal exercises are more or less accompanied with the occupation of the mind upon things. If we suppose the child to become acquainted, in the first instance, with a variety of objects, the imparting of the names is a welcome operation, and the mental fusion of each name and thing is rapidly brought about. If the objects are in any way interesting, if they arouse or excite attention, their names are eagerly embraced. On the other hand, if objects are but languidly cared for, or if they are inconspicuous or confused with other things, we are indifferent both to the things themselves and to their designations." (Alexander Bain.)

[85]"Language is the necessary tool of thought used in the conduct of the analysis and synthesis of investigation." (W. T. Harris.)

"What we are really seeking is the meaning *and* the word. One is of no value without the other in the education of the child. There is no such thing as a valuable observation and investigation of natural objects without language in which to embody the results at every step." (Geo. P. Brown.) *Report on Correlation of Studies by Committee of Fifteen*. With annotations by Geo. P. Brown.

[86]"Of course, there is great difference between the disciplinary value of that study in which the pupil solves his own difficulties and that teaching in which the teacher accompanies the pupil, supplying the needed information or suggestion at every step of his progress. The latter is not worth much for character building for the reason that it is not apt to become a part of the organized self.... The school cannot afford to expend much energy in acquiring such knowledge." (Geo. P. Brown.) *Report on Correlation of Studies by Committee of Fifteen*. With annotations by Geo. P. Brown.

[87]"In the broad view we are safe in affirming that all truth is congruous, and that truth in one department of human knowledge will always reinforce truth in any other department. There is a unity in all truth. While it is true, as Dr. Harris affirms in his Report on the Correlation of Studies, that the student does not come into the full consciousness of this fact before he attains the university, is it not also true that he can be so taught that he will *feel* this unity before he can think it, and that his feeling it will hasten the development of the power to think it?"—Geo. P. Brown, "Congruence in Teaching," *Public School Journal*, Sept., 1895.

[88]W. T. Harris.

[89]Froebel's *Letters on the Kindergarten*, page 145.

Printed in Great Britain
by Amazon